Starting with non-fiction, **Dianne Drake** penned hundreds of articles and seven books under the name JJ Despain. In 2001 she began her romance-writing career with *The Doctor Dilemma*. In 2005 Dianne's first Medical Romance, *Nurse in Recovery*, was published, and with more than 20 novels to her credit she has enjoyed writing ever since.

Also by Dianne Drake

Tortured by Her Touch
Doctor, Mummy...Wife?
The Nurse and the Single Dad
Saved by Doctor Dreamy

Deep South Docs miniseries

A Home for the Hot-Shot Doc
A Doctor's Confession

Sinclair Hospital Surgeons miniseries

Reunited with Her Army Doc
Healing Her Boss's Heart

Discover more at millsandboon.co.uk.

HEALING HER BOSS'S HEART

DIANNE DRAKE

MILLS & BOON

First published in Great Britain 2017
by Mills & Boon, an imprint of HarperCollins*Publishers*
1 London Bridge Street, London, SE1 9GF

Large Print edition 2018

ISBN: 978-0-263-07288-4

MIX
Paper from
responsible sources
FSC® C007454

This book is produced from independently certified FSC™ paper to ensure responsible forest management. For more information visit www.harpercollins.co.uk/green.

Printed and bound in Great Britain
by CPI Group (UK) Ltd, Croydon, CR0 4YY

To Bella. A cherished companion dog.

CHAPTER ONE

"YOU'RE FROM CHICAGO. Why would you choose us?" Dr. Jack Hanson stared at the blonde beauty sitting across the desk from him. She had a good physique to her. Well muscled. Looked strong. Tall. All of it suited for his program. And if facial expressions gave anything away, hers did. It screamed *determination*. This was one no-nonsense woman and, while he wasn't interested in the woman part, he was certainly intrigued by the no-nonsense.

In fact, in his own personal notes, when he'd been asked to do the recruiting for his class, the first qualification he'd listed had been no-nonsense. That, in his opinion, was a God-given trait. The rest of it could be trained into the candidates.

"The timing worked out. As I stated in my cover letter, I was asked to take a leave of absence, which may well turn into a permanent leave, and since I wasn't doing anything else, this seemed like the place for me to be. An opportunity to learn something new, maybe refocus my efforts in a new direction. That's what I do in my life, Doctor. I look for ways to move forward."

"This mandatory absence…" He folded his arms across his chest, trying to look formidable when what he was really feeling was nervous. Even before he'd started his questions, he'd discovered that she had the power to do that. He didn't know why, especially since women, in general, had no real effect on him anymore. But Carrie Kellem had marched into his broom-closet-sized office ten minutes ago, extended her hand across the desk to him, and something about the confidence in her smile had thrown him way off. So much so, he wasn't fully back yet. "You didn't explain it in full. Why not?"

"Because it's not a problem for you to worry about. My superiors think I'm too intense, too involved. Too headstrong. Because I've jumped the scene a couple more times than they're comfortable with, and they want me to step back and think about the error of my ways." She smiled. "Which isn't an error since I saved lives, and that's what I'm supposed to do."

"Explain jumping the scene."

"It means I go in before I'm ordered to."

"And you don't consider jumping the scene an error or an insubordinate move? Especially since you've said you've done it more than once? Because mountain and wilderness rescue is often slow. Painstakingly so. Sometimes it takes you hours to advance only by inches. And if you jump a scene that's not properly set for the rescue, people could get hurt. Or killed. *Including you*. So, do you have the patience for the slow procedures, and are you willing to obey orders you might not agree with? Because those are two things I need in the students I'll be admitting to the training program. In other words, I want starters, not jump-starters. Can *that* be you?"

She leaned forward, to the edge of her chair. "I'm a SWAT officer, Dr. Hanson. Specifically trained and certified as a tactical paramedic, as well. It's my job to get in and take care of anybody who's been injured during a crime in progress, or directly afterward, and if that means jumping the scene and going in before anybody else does..." She shrugged. "I'm not impatient. At least, I try not to be. Sometimes I guess I am, though, because when you see someone who needs you right that moment..." She paused, swallowed hard.

"The people who depend on me to rescue them deserve the best I can give them, and that's what they get. My best. I wouldn't be doing what I'm supposed to be doing if I'm sidelined for any reason. People could die because of that, and I don't want to be the one...responsible. When someone needs help, Doctor, that's the only thing that crosses my mind."

"Above your own safety?"

"I never even think of my own safety." She relaxed back into her chair, folded her hands in her lap, and awaited the next question.

He did like her skill level and her confidence, but it worried him that she might be too impulsive at times, which could lead to recklessness. Of course, learning to respond properly was part of his training course, so he might be able to impress on her how important it was—especially when you could be hanging off the side of a mountain—to keep everything under control and follow orders.

"But my background check on you shows that you've disobeyed orders at least three times in the past three months. In my program, and ultimately in my rescue operations, I don't tolerate that. And the people who depend on *me* to get them rescued deserve the best I can give them. So, on my team, if you can't, or won't, follow orders, you're gone. Simple as that. One screwup and you're out. Can you deal with that?"

"I can," she said, her voice as full of determination as ever, even though a little flicker of doubt wavered in her eyes.

He liked seeing that. It meant she was thinking about it—thinking about her responses, her need to take control even when it wasn't hers to have. That was good. More than that, encouraging, as she was shaping up to be the kind of rescuer he wanted. Someone with her kind of passion to help others. Someone who would do what she had to do to get the job done. Still, he did have his reservations, as Carrie seemed like she could be quite a handful, as well. Was that something he could deal with? Or even wanted to deal with?

For himself, not personally. But this wasn't personal. It was for the good of the team, and for the good of the team he *could* deal with Carrie. After all, how headstrong could she be? He glanced over at her, saw the obstinate, almost challenging look on her face, and chided himself for continuing with this interview. Because of that look… That one look told him exactly what he was going to get with her.

Yet, underneath it, did he see something vulnerable? Maybe the way she bit her lower lip. Or tried too hard to put on a swelled-up front that wasn't really her? Because she was clasping her folded hands a little too tightly. Holding herself too rigidly. Looking across at him too anxiously. He hoped that was what he was seeing, and not what he wanted to see, since that little shaving of exposure was what he was counting on.

Bottom line—he wanted her. Liked her background on her initial application. Liked her in his follow-up phone call a few weeks ago. Liked her even more now that she was here. Even with her obvious drawbacks, he saw Carrie Kellem as someone with the potential to lead her own team somewhere in the future. That's what he needed. A strong leader. Not a bunch of rescuers who could get up and down the side of a mountain without any effort, but who had the drive to put everything on the line for each and every situation.

And Carrie...he was positive she'd put it on the line. He had no doubts about that whatsoever.

"Also, I disobeyed orders four times, to be exact. You need to know the truth about me. I'm a lot of things, but I don't hide the truth. I disobeyed because I'm a trained police officer as well as a paramedic, and my job is—or was, if that turns out to be the case—taking care of people injured on a crime scene, including innocent bystanders and other cops, and sometimes I don't think it's best to wait until it's secured to go in. I can't help anybody if I'm being sidelined outside the crime scene until it's declared safe or secured. So I've disobeyed orders and gone in when I didn't have a direct order to do so."

Carrie shoved her hand through her short-cropped, almost white-blond hair and let out a frustrated breath. "If I'm entering a scene, it's because someone is bleeding, or screaming. They're in agony and their life is slipping away from them. My job is to save and rescue them any way I can." She looked over at him and suddenly her eyes went soft. "When someone needs help, they shouldn't have to wait for it. Because sometimes it comes too late. I couldn't live with myself if I was the one who could help them, but didn't, and they…"

She shook her head, shook herself out of the emotion and back into the moment. "My training, both as a special weapons and tactics police officer, as well as a tactical paramedic, qualifies me to do things that most people aren't able to do. But I must be let loose to do them. So sometimes I push the boundaries, but if a life is saved in the balance, that makes it worth the hassle I cause because I jumped in too fast."

"So you're not a team player?"

"On the contrary. I'm a great team player, but sometimes the team has to change."

"Meaning you're not always willing to follow orders?"

"I follow orders, Doctor. I can't tell you how many field rescues I've done, and I've only been reprimanded four times."

"Because you knew better than your supervisor." Yes, she was a challenge. But was she worth the challenge? Because despite her obvious problem, her supervisor had given her a strong recommendation. *Full of passion. Perfect scores in her skill tests. Dedicated.*

He was seeing all that. But he was also seeing the cautions. *She disobeys orders. She argues.*

"I'm not saying I knew better. I just saw things differently. His job was to secure the area and protect his officers, as well as innocent bystanders, on the scene. My job was to rescue injured people. We had different things to do, that's all. Basically, he thought cop first, then everything else. I though paramedic first, then cop, then everything else. Sometimes you must make hard choices if a life is hanging in the balance. And

I'm that balance, Doctor. For the person who's dying in the middle of a crime scene I'm the *only* balance, and if I'm willing to take the risk, I should be the one to make the hard choice."

Well, she was right about that. He'd spent years doing makeshift rescues in the mountains with untrained volunteers, and if that had taught him anything, it was that life was full of hard choices. He'd had to make too many of them over time. "The hard choice, until they fire you."

"I haven't been fired. They're simply…" A broad smile spread across her face. "Who am I kidding? They're not going to have me back. You know it, I know it and, most of all, they know it. This temporary suspension is their way of easing me out the door, keeping me on full benefits until I find a new position."

"But you don't seem that upset about it."

"Life moves on. You either move with it or you get left behind. I've had a lot of experience with that, and the lesson I've learned is that I *won't* get left behind. Never again."

Even with all his qualms, he liked her hang-tough attitude. She wasn't a quitter. "So, can you yank a deadweight body out?"

"Of course I can." She flexed a very well-defined bicep muscle at him. "Part of doing what I do is the training and discipline it takes every day to stay in shape. I could yank *your* deadweight body out of any situation with no problem." She grinned. "Want me to show you?"

Jack chuckled. "I think I'll pass on that but, tell me, can you put in more than your fair share of backbreaking hours? Because that's part of this. Sometimes putting aside personal life and plans. Sometimes staying out in the field until you think you can't take another step, but you know you can't quit. Can you do this? Can you accept that it may consume parts or all of your life at times?" The way it had his, until Evangeline and Alice…

"Yep," she said, her smile growing wider. "That's what I'm in it for—to do the work. Not the personal glory. I like being useful. Growing up, I never was. Never had a personal goal either, except putting myself in a position where I could make a difference."

She was so…engaging, so buoyant it was almost catching. Damn. The last thing he wanted was to be caught up by anybody's cheerfulness, but she was catching him, nevertheless. Evangeline had been so laid-back. Good, dedicated, compassionate but never up front with her feelings. Part of her Salish background. But here was Carrie, and she was a ticking time bomb of enthusiasm, ready to explode. He wasn't sure what to do about it, because it intrigued him. The women in his life were mostly from the reservation or surrounding areas—mostly like Evangeline. And while he himself wasn't a Native American, he'd practically grown up in their ways. Normal society ways mixed in with the traditional.

Ways that were not at all like Carrie's. Admittedly, Carrie's ways intrigued him. Maybe even made him a little bit nervous, because accepting Carrie would be a lot like playing with fire. And as he knew from the native ways he'd spent most of his life learning, fire was unpredictable. But it could be tamed. Yes, Carrie was fire. A basic element. And maybe fire was exactly what he needed right now…in his professional life, of course. Not in his personal. He didn't allow himself one of those anymore. "So why not be a regular paramedic and keep yourself out of the line of fire, if saving lives is all you want?"

"Somebody's got to do what I do, so why not me? Besides, I like advancing myself. Thought about being a doctor or a nurse—didn't have the time or resources to pursue any of that. But being a paramedic always intrigued me because when it's on, it's so fast-paced you must rely on your instincts, and I've always had good instincts. So when I found out there were specialties in the field…" She shrugged. "What can I say? I wanted to advance. That's who I am."

"If I accept you into my program, and you do well with it, can I count on you to stay here? Because while your need might be advancement, my need is to train qualified rescuers who will take care of the basic needs in the area."

"My life is pretty open. No one to keep me anywhere. No one place that's calling me to settle down. So I'm open to almost anything. If you think I'm good enough, and I think I'm good enough—and that's a big thing because I have to feel good enough—then there's no reason I can't stay. I don't have any ties anywhere, Doctor. So I can be tied to Marrell, Montana, as well as anywhere else."

"Well, the needs in Marrell are growing. Sinclair Hospital, the town, the population. We're attracting all kinds of outsiders who either want to build a weekend cabin or retire here. Meaning we're getting a lot of people moving in who are not used to the terrain. People who have this notion that the wild, outdoor life is for them. And they're the ones we're pulling down off mountains and ledges and out of trees. Which is why I need the best."

"You think that's me?"

"I don't think anything yet. But you've made it to the third step of the interview process, which means I see some potential. Whether you turn yourself into the best is entirely up to you. And being the best comes with a job offer."

"But if I don't like the training, or decide I don't want to pursue mountain and wilderness rescue, or if I simply don't like Marrell? Then what?"

"Then you don't stay. The rescuers I want are the ones who want to be here."

"Fair enough." She adjusted her body in the chair. Straightened her back, stretched her shoulders and frowned. "Do *you* like it here, Dr. Hanson? Like it enough to stay? Because I heard your job here is only temporary."

"I was raised near here, came back to practice after medical school, and I'm back again. So, yes, I like it. As far as being temporary goes, no. My mom married the doctor who owned the hospital, and they are semiretired. As in they'll pop back in to work when they feel the need or when we need them."

"Do you run the hospital?" she asked him.

"No, Drs. Leanne and Caleb Carsten do. But I'm the assistant chief, probably by default, since Leanne has cut back on her schedule because she's raising one child and pregnant with another, and Caleb is still on part-time status, as far as practicing goes. He was injured in Afghanistan, then injured again later, so he's in serious rehab still, which limits his doctoring abilities right now. As a result, he spends most of his time in admin work and for the next couple of weeks he's taking a break from that, rehab, because he and Leanne are in Boston, helping their son through a piano competition. He's a prodigy."

"Which leaves..."

Jack smiled. "Me, and a handful of part-timers who come in to cover various medical services."

"Sounds...hectic."

"It is, but it's good to be back." Well, parts of it were good. The rest of it...he'd just have to figure it out as he went. "And my mom was smart about how she persuaded me to come back. She knew the one thing that would keep me here would be the prospect of starting a real mountain and wilderness rescue program. It's been my passion since I was a kid and began climbing mountains So she and Henry Sinclair dangled the carrot, and I bit."

"Even though you're a surgeon?"

"Best of both worlds. Here, I'll get to do both as hospital services continue to expand."

"Sounds to me like you're happy."

If only... But Carrie didn't need to know about that gap in him, about that one thing that wouldn't let happiness in. It was his price to pay.

His burden to carry. Alone. He'd been doing it for five years now, and while it didn't get any easier over time, he'd figured out how to make it work in his life. "Anyway, tell me, why should I accept you onto my program. What do you bring that no one else will?"

"What I bring is me, and I'm pretty straightforward. I study hard, I work hard, and I'll be up for anything you want me to do."

"Until the next thing comes along?"

"Don't you, personally, always hope for the next thing?"

For a moment, he studied the challenge in her eyes. She was an arguer, a staunch defender of the way she chose to live her life, and that was another thing he liked about her. Carrie Kellem was the one who defined herself. And he wanted that—wanted her. More now than he had twenty minutes ago when she'd gone into his office announcing that she was ready to start her training—even before he'd interviewed her. "What I personally hope for is *this* best thing—my training program. Anything beyond that is on my back burner."

"So you don't look ahead?"

Or behind. Too much pain in the past. Why go back to relive it when he couldn't change it? And why look forward when, sometimes, he wasn't even sure he could make it through the current day? "What I look ahead to is in two weeks, when Caleb and Leanne are back and I'll have more time to get this program going, when I'll have seven qualified candidates sitting in my classroom, giving me their undivided attention. Other than that?" He shrugged.

"That's too bad, because there's always room to grow, Doctor. Always things you can look ahead to."

Something he'd believed once. Then had let go of.

"Now, am I accepted? You know both my strengths and weaknesses…even though I might not personally call them weaknesses. I'm sure you've talked with my former supervisors, so you know both the good and bad about me. And you also know whether you want me. So…do you?"

He did. Even though he was still wavering, Carrie had what he needed in his program. Admittedly, he wouldn't mind a little more. Maybe the edge of a friendship? Only the edge, though, because that's as far as he ever went. Except with his best friend, Palloton.

But…damn, this was tough because he wanted Carrie Kellem. With a lot of reservations. She was going to be a challenge. Maybe a problem. Still, her determination… It always went back to that. *Her determination.* He needed that most of all, and he'd never seen it so well defined in a person. Carrie embodied it, though, and that was a huge part of being a rescue specialist. Because it was a hard, isolating job, and without a huge amount of internal grit it would take a person down real fast. "I'm still thinking," he said, even though, deep down, he knew Carrie was going to make a difference to him that he wasn't sure he wanted made.

"Look, I've exhausted my options in Chicago. At least, the options I want to pursue. And so far I love everything I've seen here. It's like nothing I've ever had in my life, and the idea of waking up every morning and looking out one window and seeing wild prairie lands, then looking out another window and seeing mountains—it intrigues me, Doctor, because all I've ever known is Chicago, and buildings and street noises. And the opportunity to do my work in that wilderness or on those mountains…

"All I can be is honest. Right now, this is what I want to do. It's not my last chance, or my last resort. It's my choice. You have something I want, and I may, at some point in the future, have something you want. So accept me, or don't. It's as simple as that."

It wasn't like her to beg. But she was almost begging for this. Or coming as close to begging as she ever had. Because something about Marrell, Montana, felt right. It felt like she needed to be here. Gut instinct perhaps? Because if there was one thing she'd learned to do at an early age, it was to trust her gut. Sometimes it was the only thing that had saved her.

He chuckled. "You drive a hard bargain, Carrie."

Her eyes crinkled into a warm smile. The smile

of victory. "I know. That's what makes me so irresistible."

"Well, irresistible isn't what I'm looking for. It's strength of mind and character, and the willingness to work harder than you've ever worked in your life."

"A few months back I had a hostage who was down, bleeding out from multiple gunshot wounds inside a bank that was being held up. Three gunmen in total. They didn't want him to die because they didn't want to face murder charges, so I got to him pretty easily. They let me in. Met me with a gun in my back. Told me to fix him, then get him out of there. And here's this nearly three-hundred-pound man who didn't want to go because he was afraid if I jostled him, he'd bleed to death.

"So, I've got a gun at my back and this belligerent man resisting everything I was trying to do. My only hope was to sneak in a sedative and wait until it took him down enough that I could drag him out into the street.

"Trust me, he wasn't easy. I ended up with a broken nose, a sprained wrist and more bruises than I could count. But today he's alive and well and embellishing his story on his radio sports talk show every chance he gets. *He* was the hardest work I've ever had. So if you've got something harder, bring it on. I'm ready for it."

"Well, try doing that dangling on the end of a rope extended out over a six-thousand-foot drop, then we'll talk."

She laughed. "OK, so you've got me beat. But let me just say this. The reason you should let me into your program is that, so far, my life has been all about getting myself to a place that's more of a challenge than the last place I was. I take the risks. I meet the challenges. But I also get the results. If you give me this opportunity—and you know you want to—you stand a fair chance of getting exactly what you want out of this program." This time when she smiled at him she wrinkled her nose. She hadn't meant to because it came so close to…flirting. And she didn't flirt. Never flirted. Never wanted to find herself in the position of having to deal with the results. Yet she'd just wrinkled her nose…

"Which would be…?"

"Me," she said. "And all my experience."

"You, the person who doesn't follow orders. So, tell me. How am I going to deal with that? Because there's no room for it in my program."

"Sounds like you've just accepted me."

"Maybe I have."

"In that case, all I can say is I'll try to do better. I want this. I don't want to go over the top and ruin my chances. So I'll do everything I can to make sure I don't."

"Won't that be fighting the natural woman? Because I see what you're made of, and I'm not sure you *can* fight it."

"Then accept me provisionally, or put me on probation. I want this. I want to be in a place where I'm needed. Where I can make a difference. And I can do that here—for you."

"Not *for me*, Carrie. For the people who'll need you. But you're tempting me. I'm concerned, though, that we've got all kinds of experience here you've never had. Mountains, rivers, wilderness, wildlife..." He shrugged. "Since you've always been a city girl, you won't be afraid to take it on, will you?"

"Nothing's ever scared me." Not since the night they'd taken her away from her mother and thrown her in a foster home for her own benefit. Her mom had been a drunk. A drug addict. And Carrie remembered lying on the cot in the large room full of other scared kids, listening to so many of them cry. She'd cried, too, that night. She'd become one of the many. But she'd been old enough to realize that she couldn't be just one of the many if she wanted to survive. She couldn't be scared. Couldn't cry. And after that night she hadn't allowed anything to scare her. She shook her head, clenched her jaw. "No, it doesn't scare me."

"You do realize you probably wouldn't have the opportunity to join the police force here. At least, not in the same capacity as in Chicago."

"That's fine. I want to be a paramedic first anyway. I only went through police training so I could specialize as a tactical paramedic, and it was required of me. Of course, if becoming the town sheriff or anything comes with a horse and a cowboy hat..."

"Nope. He drives a mountain-worthy SUV

and, as far as I know, the only hat I've ever seen him in is a bright orange stocking cap he wears when he's out in the woods."

"Well, I don't look good in orange, so I may have to find some other kind of work here to help me support myself. Maybe something part-time in your emergency department. If there's an opening."

"Well, like I already said, I do have some concerns. I'll be honest about that. But if you can keep your over-exuberance under control, you're in. The term is eight weeks for the initial part of the training, at least forty hours a week, with continuing education follow-ups until you're certified. You'll be on call for any and all emergencies during your training. The assignments will be my choice, not yours. So, do you want this?"

"I let my apartment go back in Chicago, sold my furniture to get me out here and get me set up so, yes, I want this. Now, can my dog get some training on this course along with me?"

"You have a dog?"

"Big one, with a good tracking sense. Smart.

Trains easily. I've always thought she'd be great in the field."

Jack dropped his head back against the chair and let out a long sigh. "You're going to insist on the dog, aren't you?"

"Well, maybe not insist so much as try to persuade. There can be advantages."

He stared straight at her. "You never quit, do you?"

She smiled, feeling as happy about this new opportunity as she'd ever felt about anything. "Never."

Jack's response was to groan. Simply groan, then shut his eyes.

CHAPTER TWO

CARRIE HANDED A dog treat to Bella, her large, black Labrador-mutt mix, and climbed into the pickup truck next to her, nudging Bella back over to the passenger's side. "We're in," she said to her companion. Bella and Carrie had been together for a year now, resulting from an unintentional meeting. Bella had gotten caught up in some gunfire—an innocent passerby—and had taken a bullet to her hindquarter. Nothing serious—just a flesh wound. But she'd needed patching, and Carrie happened to be the one on the scene who could do that. Only problem was, after she'd dropped Bella off at the closest veterinarian's office for better care, the bill had come to her since Bella was a stray. So, because she'd paid for the dog's care, she'd kept the dog. Best thing she'd ever done. "He seems nice enough. Not very personable, but we're not here to make friends, are we?" she asked her friend, as she eased her truck forward and started off down Marrell's main street toward the one-room garage apartment she was renting.

By the time she reached her temporary home. Carrie was more than ready to go inside, kick back and spend the evening reading a medical journal. Maybe open a can of soup and heat it up over a single burner hot plate and snuggle in. She hadn't expected to live in the lap of luxury, coming to Montana, but she'd hoped for something better than this. One room, a foldout sofa that converted to a bed, a tiny kitchen table for two with a wobbly leg, a chair. But it was warm, and given that it was almost October, and she'd already been caught up in light snow flurries, that warmth was a bonus. That, plus the fact that there was a little stretch of open land across the road where she could walk Bella without having to go too far.

"There's no place to go," she said, adjusting her cell phone to speaker so she could get comfortable talking to her former roomie, Hannah Clarkson. Hannah was a nurse practitioner who managed a small satellite clinic for one of Chicago's leading hospitals. "I knew I'd be getting into some pretty remote areas, but I didn't expect it to be quite so…isolated."

"Have you made any friends?" Hannah asked.

"I don't want to make any friends. I'm here to work hard, get through the program and figure out what's next. The doctor in charge is already offering me a job here—well, almost—so who knows. If things work out…"

"Is he sexy?"

Leave it to Hannah to cut to the bottom line. "To you, maybe. He's tall, well built. Rugged. But I'm not looking for sexy." Dredging up a quick mental recall of Dr. Jack Hanson, she decided he was, indeed, sexy. Nice muscles. Strong. She especially liked the three-day growth of stubble on his face. His longish dark brown hair. His charcoal eyes. OK, maybe she'd been too long without a man in her life since just picturing him gave her a little tingle. But having a man, or not having one, had never been her focus. And she wasn't about to make that any kind of a focus now.

"You're not looking, period. Remember that firefighter…what was his name?"

"Um…I don't remember." Actually, she did. And he'd been a hunk and a half. And caught up in one of those complicated situations halfway between married and divorced. In her life, there was never room for anything complicated so she'd moved on. But that was going on to two years ago now, and she'd never had a date since. Even then, their dates hadn't really been dates. More like chance encounters. A few minutes here, a few there. Nothing special.

"Liar," her friend accused. "He was great."

"He was thinking about going back to his wife."

"OK, maybe he was a bad choice. But how will you ever know a good choice if you don't allow yourself to look?"

"I'll look. Just not right now."

"Well, all I'm saying is keep your options open. You owe yourself a little fun. And a future outside your job."

A future outside her job? The words rattled around in her brain long after she'd quit talking to Hannah. And, they scared her, because she was good at her job. Felt safe in it. But outside it…what had she ever had that was worth anything? Had there ever been anything in life that had made her feel safe? No, there hadn't.

Well, Hannah may have been right about some things, but changing herself was easier said than done. Her life had always been about survival, and when you lived only to survive, everything else took a back seat. Quite honestly, she didn't know any other way to live. Mentally and emotionally—sure, there was more to it, and she envied the people she could see having that kind of life. But for Carrie survival mode always took over. In and out of foster homes from the age of five until she was sixteen. Then bumped out to the street, living on her own, by her wits. Eating out of trash bins, avoiding the bad people, the bad influences. Always wanting more. Always knowing that if she could find the way, she could have it. Always fighting to get ahead and never giving up. That's who she was because she didn't know how to be anything else.

Glumly, Carrie set aside her soup and put Bella

on her lead, then walked over to the field and simply stood there as Bella sniffed around, then pulled her in different directions, investigating all her options. For her dog, it was an easy thing. Find it then follow it. But for her, that had always hurt. Too many times over her growing-up years she'd thought she'd found it, only to be turned away. She'd had to become hard to survive. She'd had to become disengaged to keep from getting hurt. Problem was she didn't know how to engage now. At thirty-three she didn't have a clue.

"Too many years alone," she said to Bella, as they headed back to the apartment a little while later. "Sort of like the way you were when I found you. Alone, wounded." Except Bella's wounds had healed. Carrie's, on the other hand, had not. They were too deep. Too ingrained in who she was. "Part and parcel," she said, leading Bella up the stairs. "That which has to be accepted as part of something else." Or, in other words, as part of her.

Once inside, Carrie debated returning to her reading or stretching out on the lumpy sofa bed. The bed won, so she stripped down to her undies, climbed in, pulled the blanket up over her and shut her eyes, even though she wasn't the least bit tired or sleepy. But sleeping beat staying awake, thinking about her place in life. Something she was prone to doing too often.

And ten seconds later thoughts of Jack Hanson flashed across her mind. She tingled a little, unwilling recollections skittering across her mind. His body—the muscles. His eyes—so intense. And the smile that didn't come easily, but when it did was so…warm. Inviting. She rubbed her arms against the goose bumps coming to life. All over an image in her head. Men didn't affect her that way. She didn't let them. But the more she thought about Jack, and the more she tingled, the more her goose bumps marched up and down.

Sighing, she turned on her side, hoping a new position would bring on different thoughts. But it didn't work as Jack was still playing with her. She didn't really know anything about him. He was gruff, which she didn't mind. Very direct, which attracted her. And dedicated. Maybe that was his best quality. She liked dedication. Liked someone with a purpose, a destination, and it seemed that Jack had both.

He wasn't married, she finally decided, after turning over to her other side, realizing she was fighting a losing battle. Jack would leave her mind in his own good time, and there wasn't much she could do to control it. No, not married…at least, he didn't wear a wedding band. No trace of one either. And there was nothing else about him to indicate he was.

His appearance was a little unkempt, in a rugged way. Didn't have a wife's finishing touch. Or what she thought should be a wife's touch. What she'd do if she were a wife. But was he involved? Did he get involved or was he a player? "No," she said, still trying to force the thought of him from her head as she climbed out of bed, headed to the sink for a drink of water, and was interrupted partway across the room with the *"Eine Kleine Nachtmusik"* jingle of her cell phone.

"Kellem here," she said, when her caller ID failed to note who was on the other end.

"Jack Hanson." Simple response. No embellishments.

"What can I do for you, Dr. Hanson?" she asked, not sure what to make of a call coming in at nearly eleven o'clock.

"We have a medical situation. You mentioned that you might want to take a part-time job as a paramedic. So, if that's the case, you're hired."

"A case? As in?"

"Priscilla Anderson, one of our senior residents, is having a heart episode—not sure if it's an attack or what—and she can't get to us, so we need to get to her. I'm in my truck, I've got your address, and I'm two minutes away. Be ready. It's going to be a hike, so be ready for that, too. Oh, and that garage you're living above…there's a better apartment over Millie's Diner. A little more room, not as run-down. Probably safer."

"And more expensive. This place is fine. Easy on the budget."

"Suit yourself. But if you change your mind…" With that, he clicked off, leaving Carrie standing there, practically naked, staring at the phone, like that was going to give her more information. Which, of course, it didn't. So, three minutes later, she ran down the outside steps of her apartment and straight to the pickup truck parked in front of it. With Bella at her heels.

"You're not bringing that dog, are you?" Jack grumbled, instead of greeting her with a "Hello" or "Glad you could make it." Or even doing the polite thing by opening the truck door for her.

"She won't get in the way."

"She'll stay in the truck," he said, as he gunned the engine, and the tires spun briefly on the icy road before they caught traction and the three of them were on their way.

"She's had obedience training, and she carries my supplies. Assuming you've brought supplies for me to carry."

"I have." Jack glanced over at the dog, who'd managed to find her spot between Carrie and him. "And you expect her to carry them in that red pack she's wearing?"

"Frees me up to take in additional equipment, if needed. Or, when I was working SWAT, carry a gun."

"They let you take her in?"

"Nobody ever stopped me. Although I never put her in harm's way. If there was gunfire, she stayed in the car." She glanced over at Jack, saw the grim set of his face, and scooted back in her seat but didn't relax. "So, why me tonight?"

"You were free."

"You've got other students in town who could do just as well."

"But, as I said, we've got some hiking to do, and you seemed like the one to do it."

"Do you always make house calls?" she asked him.

"When I have to. In areas like this, you do whatever it takes. Tonight it's going to take a half-mile hike up a steep trail, because the road that winds up to Priscilla's place is iced over and not safe to drive."

"So, how do we know it's a heart *episode*?"

"That's what she said when she phoned me. And she only calls for help if she thinks it's serious, so I have no reason to doubt she got it wrong. Symptoms fit. She has a history of mild heart disease. Asthma, too." He elbowed Bella back toward Carrie. "Look, I'm not happy that you're bringing the dog, but since she's here there's nothing I can do about it. So, please, keep her off my lap and don't let her lean on me. Or drool on me."

"You don't like dogs?"

"One thing you'll discover about me the further into training you get is that I'm not always the most tolerant person. Fair warning. I'm good at what I do, but sometimes I'm not the nicest person to be around."

"Any particular reason for that?" she asked.

He shrugged. "I try to keep myself focused on my work, and I'm not good with distractions. Like dogs. Personally, I like them well enough. Just not with me on a house call."

And that was the last thing he said until he brought the truck to a stop on a winding, narrow road and hopped out. "Your supplies are behind the seat. Put them in the doggie bag, if that's what you want to do. And stay as close to me as you can, because you don't know the area, the path is going to be slick, and I don't want you getting hurt."

"Guess we'd better hurry," she said, slinging her bag of supplies over her shoulder, then scrambling along after him, trying to stay close enough that she could benefit from the flashlight he shone on the trail ahead of him.

While she didn't know much about mountain rescue yet, she did know that the last thing she needed was to be out on a mountain trail, in the cold, after dark, lost and alone. Not that he would care. Or even notice. Because, from her little corner of the world, it seemed that Jack Hanson wasn't the type of person who got himself caught up in anything other than his work, the same way she didn't. Which made him a perfect match for her—medically speaking.

She liked that. In fact, she got excited about it as, outside her training, she'd never worked with anyone before. Always alone on the job. With backup, of course. But the medical duty had been up to her, and there had been no one there beside her to help.

Now that Jack was practically her first partner, it felt nice. Gave her a different kind of confidence, as if, because of him, she could do more. Do better. Even the thought of watching his hands work—gentle hands, she assumed—gave her a little jolt. Competent hands. The hands of a skilled lover… No— She wasn't going there. That was way too far. *Mind on the job, Carrie*, she warned herself. She had to keep her mind only on the medical and not on the other potential non-medical skills of Jack's hands.

"What do we do when we get there? How do we get her out, since we can barely get in?" she asked, hoping he didn't notice the smidgen of wobbliness in her voice.

"I've got a couple of volunteers coming in behind us, about an hour out, if we're lucky, and they'll help us get her back to the truck. After that…" He paused, turned to shine the light on her face. "She's my grandmother. I've got an airlift on standby if she's too bad to keep at Sinclair. Which makes her one of the lucky ones, because I can afford to do it. But there are hundreds of people living out here who don't get that benefit. Which is why we need to get in to them better than we're able to do now. Give them a quicker response, an earlier intervention."

"Your grandmother lives out here alone?" That surprised her, as she'd never known anyone who lived so remotely. Even in her worst days, living in alley doorways, she'd been surrounded by civilization. But to live so far out… It wasn't exactly an unappealing idea. A scary one, but one she might have to get used to if Jack hired her after the program was finished.

"Always has. She homesteaded the area with my grandfather, and stayed on after he died. Won't leave. Stubborn, like you are."

"But she gets to Marrell occasionally?"

"When she wants, which isn't very often. She lives life on her own terms, and nothing's going to change that."

Like Jack? she wondered. Because he, too, seemed like he lived life on his own terms. "So, what's the plan after we get there?" she asked, fighting hard to keep up with him as he turned back to the trail and doubled his pace. He was strong. Had huge hiking skills, the likes of which she'd never seen before. And, for the first time, she got a good sense of what he wanted out of his program. Saw the vital necessity of it.

"We're going to stabilize her for transport. That's all we're equipped for right now. Get an IV going, get her on oxygen, give her cardiac meds if she needs them, and kick the wall and curse because we can't do more." He slowed just slightly. Not enough to make much of a difference, but enough so it gave Carrie a chance to almost catch up to him. But before she did completely, he started off again as fast and furiously as before. "And feed her cats. She's got a bunch of them, and she's more worried about them than she is about herself. Hope your dog is OK with cats."

"Her name is Bella and, yes, she's fine with cats."

On hearing her name, Bella bounded in front of Carrie on the trail, leaving Carrie the last in line, feeling like a real slacker. Even though she prided herself on being physically fit, she had nothing on Jack Hanson, and it was easy to see that she was going to have to do better. Back in Chicago, she'd been proud of being the fittest one on her team. Here, in Marrell, she wondered if she even amounted to average.

"Well, *she* stays outside once we get there. I don't want her getting in the way," he said as he veered off the main path to the left, and totally disappeared in the dark for a moment.

"Dr. Hanson?" Carrie called out, not so much from being afraid of the dark, or being lost in it, but from the uncertainty of which way to go.

He spun around and flashed the light directly in her eyes. "Name's Jack. Nobody's very formal in Marrell."

"And when we're in class?" she asked, finally catching all the way up to him.

"Sir will be fine," he said, taking hold of her arm and leading her off the path entirely.

Despite herself, she laughed. "You don't have an inflated opinion of yourself, do you?" Up ahead, beyond a dense thicket of early-winter undergrowth, she could see the glowing lights from the cabin she assumed to be their destination. The house didn't appear large, but it seemed… cozy. Something she'd always wanted for herself at some point in her life. Far, far down the line, if ever, she supposed.

"Of course I don't," he said, his voice full of a humor that was impossible to see in the dark.

But was there, nonetheless. "But in my case, if I did, my opinion would be justified."

Carrie laughed again, as they finally made it out of the trees and picked up speed across a lawn that was littered with snow-dusted gnomes and elves and flamingos she assumed to be pink. "You don't bring your crown on house calls, do you?"

"My crown is always implied," he said, as he stepped up onto the front porch, its wooden planks swathed in a dim yellow light. "As you'll soon come to realize." Then he opened the door. "Priscilla," he called out, to which six or seven cats responded with a variety of meows.

She liked his sarcastic humor. It was…sexy, in an offbeat way. Kept her on her toes, made her think. She liked the way his niceness slipped in when he was trying so hard to keep it out, too. Trying so hard to be a grump. But he wasn't grumpy. Not really. A little preoccupied, often totally focused, sometimes distracted. That really wasn't grumpy, though. More like concerned or concentrated. Not fond of being interrupted in the moment. The way she was, come to think of it. Sometimes she would ignore someone or snap when someone interrupted her, but that wasn't grumpy, the way Jack wasn't grumpy when he did the same. Then there was his competence—it radiated from him. He was very calculated in what he did, didn't waste time or effort, but he was methodical. And to her even that was sexy. In fact, the whole aura surrounding him was sexy. He was perverse, intense, maybe a little dark at times, but there was nothing wrong with that. Not personally. Not professionally. All in all, Carrie liked Jack Hanson. Not for a deeply personal relationship, since he was giving off absolutely no vibes in that direction, but maybe in a situation she would loosely define as a casual friendship. And the thought of him as her friend while she was here in Marrell—she liked that. It could work. If his crown didn't get in the way.

Priscilla Anderson was sitting on the edge of her bed, looking like she was ready for a hike down the mountain. Probably something well north of seventy, she looked twenty years younger, all decked out in jeans and a red plaid jacket, with her long white hair pulled back into a ponytail. "Just let me get my boots on and I'll be ready to go back down with you," she said.

"How?" Jack asked, as Carrie sprang to action, checking the woman's vital signs. "Your road's icing over, and I'm going to be lucky to get volunteers in, let alone get you out of this damned isolated shack."

"It may be a shack, Jackie Hanson, but it's all mine. Which is more than I can say for that *shack* you're living in. Willard Mason's old run-down piece of trash. No running water, no toilet..."

"It has water, it has plumbing. And electricity. All the modern conveniences..."

"Which you had to pay to have put in."

"Because I bought the place." He bent to give his grandmother an affectionate peck on the cheek, then shoved one of her cats aside so he could sit next to her. "So, when did the pain start?"

"It's not exactly a pain. More like a heavy sensation. And it started three hours ago. I'd have called you sooner, but I was hoping it was indigestion and it would go away."

"Well, it didn't." He took hold of Priscilla's wrist to take her pulse. Then looked up at Carrie. "Fast, but not thready." Then he looked into his grandmother's eyes, took out his stethoscope, listened to her lungs. When he went for her chest, though, she swatted away his hand.

"Let *her* do that," she snapped, nodding to Carrie. "Don't want you touching me so privately. Not respectable for a grandson to be doing that."

"When did *you* become such a prude, old woman?" Jack said, standing up and stepping back from the bed, which allowed Carrie to get closer, check Priscilla's heart and take her blood pressure.

"The day I heard you were taking over here as a doctor." She looked up at Jack, and actually winked. "Scary stuff, Jackie, for an old woman who used to powder your behind."

"Blood pressure's a little elevated," Carrie interjected, looking first at Priscilla, then at Jack. "Heartbeat's strong, but tachy, like you said. I counted one-forty."

"Who's she, by the way?" Priscilla nodded

toward Carrie, but didn't look directly at her. "Your nurse?"

"Nope. Her name's Carrie. She's one of my new students," Jack said as he pulled an IV setup out of his backpack and continued to talk as he worked. "From Chicago. A paramedic. Highly trained in dealing with people as stubborn as you. Oh, and she carries a gun."

Priscilla arched appreciative eyebrows. "Well, good for you, Carrie. I've always admired a woman who could shoot."

"Only on the job, Mrs. Anderson," Carrie told her. "I'm a cop. Guns come with the territory. Out here, though, no guns. The only weapon I have is a wooden spoon that comes with the apartment I'm renting. I don't do guns on my own time. Don't even own a personal one."

"Me either. Best weapon I've got is my brain. Use it wisely and I can get everything I want. Like a grandson who makes house calls in the middle of the night. Oh, and call me Priscilla. Mrs. Anderson is too formal."

"Because I want to persuade you to move to town. To move in with me."

Priscilla winked at Carrie. "Jackie seems to think he knows what's best for me. Always has. Most of the time I just indulge him. It makes him feel better."

"Then indulge me now," Jack said. "Just say yes, and by the time I get you out of the hospital, I'll have a room ready for you."

"And my cats?" She looked up at Carrie again. "See, that's the question I always ask him when he brings it up, because he won't take the cats, and I won't go without them. So this is where he shuts up about moving me and gets back to business."

"This time, back to business means…" He waved an IV catheter at her.

"You're not sticking *that* in me," Priscilla warned him.

"If I have to tie you down, I will," he said, pointing to the pillow at the head of her bed. "Now, jacket off, feet up, head where it belongs. And stick out your arm."

"Don't trust you as far as I can see you," she grumbled, doing exactly what he said. "Never have." She looked at Carrie. "No compassion for his elders," she said.

Except compassion was all Carrie saw. It was touching, and sweet. *Sweet*—a word she was sure he wouldn't like attached to him. But he was, and it was lovely to watch. He loved his grandmother dearly, and it showed in everything he was doing. It especially showed in the worry written all over his face. And seeing that worry—she fell in love a little bit. Not in the happily-ever-after sense, but in the sense that Jack had qualities she'd never seen in any of the men in her life, and she loved seeing them in him. Loved knowing a gentler side than she'd ever seen in another man—not that there'd ever been a significant man in her life, because there hadn't been. But the ones she'd known—users, for the most part. Not Jack, though. She could tell he was a giver.

She'd never had that in her life, never had someone love her the way Priscilla loved Jack either. Or the way Jack loved Priscilla. It was nice. Gave her hope that it might be out there for her, someday.

* * *

There was something about this place—all the time he'd spent here growing up, the things his grandmother had taught him here, bringing Evangeline and Alice here… Priscilla had loved Alice deeply and dearly. They'd had a special bond. The same bond he'd shared with his grandmother when he'd been Alice's age. Walks through her garden, fresh-baked chocolate-chip cookies, and the stories… Nobody told better stories than Priscilla and he could almost see Alice and Priscilla sitting together on the floor, Alice's brown Salish eyes wide with amazement as Priscilla told the tales of her childhood, or her own adventures in Saka'am, when she'd go to visit friends. It hurt. All of it hurt now. The memories. And images. He wanted them back the way they used to be, not the way they were now.

Except he couldn't have that because everything was shrouded in grief and sorrow. That picture of Alice—the one where she and Priscilla were wading in the stream, drenched from a spill or two, looking all sloppy and wet and happy—Jack knew his grandmother had put it away because he couldn't bear to look at it. Because it broke his heart when he did. And that afghan Evangeline had spent months crocheting—nowhere to be seen. Bits and pieces of his past all tucked away so he wouldn't be reminded, but everything reminded him. Dragged him back to those days. To his wife. Especially to his daughter. "Oh, I have compassion," he finally said in response. "I save it up for those who deserve it."

"And I don't deserve it?" Priscilla asked, pretending to be outraged.

"What you deserve is for me to come in here, throw you over my shoulder, and carry you down that mountain, like it or not."

"Not," Priscilla practically shouted. "And I'll have you arrested—"

"You know, every family has one—the crazy relative nobody talks about," he said to Carrie as he gave his grandmother's hand a squeeze, once the IV was in place. "Well, this is the one who belongs to *my* family." He bent and kissed Priscilla's cheek.

"Never had a family, so never had the pleasure," she told him.

Priscilla laughed, and reached over to pat Jack's hand. "Well, my Jackie here is available. I'd die a happy woman if he could find someone again."

Again? Carrie raised her eyebrows, but didn't ask, much to Jack's relief. "Except you're not going to die," Jack reassured her, as a telltale red started creeping from his neck to his face. He didn't talk about Evangeline. Or Alice. *Ever*. And people who knew him knew better than to speak of her. "And I'm not looking to find someone. So, no more talking. I want you to save your energy for the trip back to Sinclair."

"I know why you don't want me talking, Jackie, and it has nothing to do with going to Sinclair. But I'll cooperate." With that, she pretend-zipped her lips, lay back into her pillows and shut her eyes.

"She's pouting," Jack said to Carrie, the red still evident. "Thinks it gains her some sympathy."

"Well, I'm sympathetic." Carrie sat down on the other side of the bed, then took Priscilla's hand. "And for your information, Jack, I like your grandmother. I like her spunk and her attitude. You're a lucky man to have her."

"That's what I keep telling him," Priscilla interjected, opening her eyes. "So, when do we ride, Jackie? Because if I must do this, I want to get it over with so I can get back home to my cats."

"Soon, Priscilla," he said, feeling as helpless as he had the night his wife and daughter had died. Helpless, angry, and damned ready to kick in that wall. "Got a couple of people on the way up right now to help carry you out."

"You can't carry me?" she asked, her voice weakening.

"Too dangerous. Carrie's not experienced on the mountain, and I can't do it by myself..."

"He climbs like a mountain goat. Did he tell you that, Carrie? Jackie climbs like he was born on the side of a mountain. Taught him everything he knows about it."

"You climbed?" Carrie asked her.

"Up until the arthritis got me a few years back. In fact, Jackie and I had a lot of good times together. He was a natural on the ropes. Liked to free-climb, too. Not me, though. I was always a little more cautious. So, do you climb at all, Carrie?"

"Never have. But I'm going to learn."

"Good for you," Priscilla closed her eyes again, this time finally succumbing to exhaustion. "Jackie likes his women strong. Likes 'em keeping up with him."

"But I'm not—" she started to protest, then stopped. No point. Priscilla was sound asleep, her head leaning on Jack's shoulder, and Jack's arm around her, supporting her.

"She's one tough old bird," Jack said affectionately, as he took her pulse.

"A tough old bird who taught you how to rock climb." Carrie broke away from Priscilla to check the drip of the IV.

"That, and other wilderness survival skills. She's been a midwife of sorts for more than fifty years. There probably isn't a mountain within forty miles of here she hasn't climbed at one time or another, trying to help in a medical situation. People around here trust her, probably more than they've ever trusted my mom and me, and we're both doctors." Probably a whole lot more than he'd trusted himself as, for the past five years, he hadn't had a lot of that going on.

The trip down the mountain wasn't as bad as he'd anticipated. Help had arrived, they'd carried Priscilla to his truck, and while the ride to the hospital was interminably long due to road conditions and safety concerns, three hours after getting to his grandmother, she was safely tucked into a hospital bed, with an IV drip in her arm and heart monitor leads stuck to her chest, fussing that she was feeling fine and she wanted to go home to her cats.

"She's stubborn," Carrie commented, as she passed by Jack, who was seated in the chair across from Priscilla's bed, on her way to fill the bedside pitcher with water.

"And proud of it," Priscilla said, even though her eyes were closed.

Jack glanced up at the heart monitor over her bed, glad it was reading normal. Glad that Carrie had been there to help him through this.

But, most of all, glad that Carrie had met his every expectation of her as a medic. He didn't always have a lot of patience with the people who worked with him. They were too slow to suit him. Or, didn't have a technique or bedside manner he liked. But Carrie had been…perfect. She'd known exactly what to say, and do. And, most of all, she'd gained his grandmother's trust, which wasn't an easy thing to do, as Priscilla hated modern medicine. "Aren't you supposed to be sleeping, old woman?" he asked, his eyes stuck on Carrie as she carried the water back to the bedside stand.

"How am I supposed to sleep when you're hovering over me the way you are?"

"I'm not hovering," he said, giving Carrie a wink. "I'm just being a good doctor and watching over my patient."

"Which is the same thing as hovering. So, go hover somewhere else." She opened her eyes, reached over and squeezed Carrie's hand. "And you, young lady, look like you could do with some sleep."

"So she gets to sleep while I have to go hover?"

Jack asked, as he pushed himself to his feet, then walked over to the bed. He bent over and kissed Priscilla on the cheek. "You take care of yourself tonight, Priscilla," he said. "And call me if you need anything. I'm ten minutes away."

"I'm fine, Jackie," she said. "Just had a little scare."

"Which gave me a big scare. Now—sleep." With that, he took hold of Carrie's hand and led her from the room. Once in the hall, he slumped against the wall, shut his eyes and simply stood there for a minute before he said anything. "If anything happened to her, I don't know what..." He opened his eyes and stopped. He was revealing too much of himself. He'd almost allowed Carrie into places no one was allowed. But she was easy to talk to, to be around. Which meant, he was going to have to be more careful. "Look, Carrie. I appreciate you going out there with me. Priscilla can be difficult at times, and the way you were with her...again, I appreciate it."

"Why do you call her Priscilla, and not Grandmother or Grandma?" she asked.

He chuckled. "When I was young, she made

me call her Mrs. Anderson. Said it was all about proper respect. It wasn't until I was about fourteen or fifteen that she let me call her by her first name. She said I'd earned that right." Carrie had earned that right immediately. He was impressed, as Priscilla was a hard person to reach out to. But Carrie had reached out and touched. Which made him feel…good. Yes, he felt very, very good about Carrie. Maybe that even went a little beyond her medical skills. He felt good about her in general.

CHAPTER THREE

"NO, I'M FINE," Carrie said, trying to ignore the well-intentioned nurse who'd decided to take Carrie under her wing and turn her into a happy woman. Got to be married, got to be in a relationship. That was all she'd heard from Georgia Hobbs since her first day on the job. This was day five now, and Georgia hadn't given up. She had an available nephew. A son. And a next-door neighbor's son. All of them just looking for someone.

"I appreciate your invitation, but I've got to study tomorrow evening, to get myself ready for my class."

Besides, she didn't feel like trying to be social with someone she didn't know and didn't seem to have anything in common with other than work. So, while Carrie was grateful for the invitation to dinner, she simply wasn't interested in what was being offered. She didn't date. Didn't want to get back in the habit again. At least, not now. Not when there were more important things in her future.

Georgia blew out a frustrated breath. "Do you even know anybody here in Marrell?"

She knew Jack a little bit. In the few days she'd been here, they'd had a casual coffee once. And joined in with a group from the hospital who'd gone out for a beer after work. But that was all, and it was fine. It worked. They were friendly, but not friends. "I don't really have time," she said, trying to edge her way out of the entrance door and find a place to hide in the storage room, or anyplace else Georgia might not be so inclined to look for her.

"We're going into winter pretty soon, and it can get depressing if you're here all by yourself. No friends. No one to go out and grab a pizza with. You start feeling…shut in."

She'd spent a lifetime feeling shut in, in one way or another. Why should this be any different? "I'm really not interested," Carrie emphasized, then sidestepped away from the entry, hoping Georgia wouldn't follow. But she did. And persisted.

"I was a stranger here once, Carrie. I know what it's like being alone in a new place."

"I've been on my own for a long time, Georgia." That was why she took on independence with a vengeance. She didn't want to depend on somebody else for her life. There was no stability in that and, above all, Carrie wanted stability. Or, at least, a little piece of it. "And while I appreciate your concern, there's nothing to be concerned about. Like I said, I'm fine."

"Well, in case you change your mind..." Georgia shook her head, not so much annoyed as perplexed. "Just let me know. Promise?"

"Promise," Carrie said grudgingly, then turned and almost ran toward the supply closet, where she stepped inside, shut the door behind her, and leaned against the door. At least in Chicago no one had bothered her. No one had cared. No one had come after her, trying to fix her. As if being single was something to fix. She was fine as she was. Well suited for her life. Steeled against the pain and disappointment of getting too close, only to be rejected.

And, she wasn't about to let Georgia, or anybody else, make her feel guilty for her choices, or force her into a change she didn't want to make, so she could fit in better. Truth was, she'd never fit in anywhere, and now she didn't care if she never did.

"You OK in there?" A familiar voice seeped through the door. "Saw you come in, thought you'd come right back out, but it's been five minutes, and since there's nothing worth spending five minutes on in the closet..."

"I'm fine," she said, still not giving up her spot against the door.

"Need some help?"

"Nope, I'm good."

"Got time for a cup of coffee?" he asked. "There's something I want to discuss with you. Privately. In my office."

"About the school?" She was not quite ready to accept his invitation, yet not quite ready to turn it down either. Because the idea of a little one-on-one with him did raise her heartbeat a notch or two, as it had previously during their few times together. But it was something she always wrote off as nervousness due to her new direction in her career path.

"Come out and I'll tell you. It's something I think you might enjoy. You and that dog of yours."

"Bella. Her name's Bella." Carrie stepped away from the door, then opened it, but didn't emerge into the hall. Rather, she stood in the doorway and looked up at him. She tried not to get herself caught up in how good he looked in his green scrubs, stethoscope slung casually around his neck. A couple of days' growth of beard. Hair mussed. He was a handsome man by any definition of the word...and just because she didn't date them it didn't mean she couldn't look, and enjoy.

Unfortunately, she got caught up too quickly, too easily. "Did you say coffee?" she asked, to diffuse the moment. Or the imaginary moment that was trying to pop into her mind. The one where she hadn't stepped into the hall for him, but he'd stepped into the closet for her... *Just let it go,* she chided herself, forcing her eyes to the clock on the wall behind him. "Because I've got a break coming up and…"

"Yes, coffee," he said, his expression perfectly impassive. Then followed immediately with, "What's got you so spooked? You seem jumpy."

She smiled. Not spooked as much as affected. He did that to her. He *affected* her. "People around want to…" She exaggerated a cringe. "Fix me up. You know, introduce me to brothers, nephews and cousins."

A seductive eyebrow arched and a half smile crossed his lips. "And you don't like that?"

"Don't like it, don't want it. Never have. Never will. It's not my style."

"What *is* your style, Carrie Kellem?" he asked, turning to head down the hall, presumably to his office.

Carrie followed, but kept her distance for fear that, if they walked shoulder to shoulder, one of the do-gooders would read something into it that wasn't there. "I don't really have a *style*. More like a philosophy. I was a late starter in life. Never really had a sense of who I was or where

I belonged. And the result is, because I never fit in before, I don't have an overpowering urge to fit in anywhere in the present or even the future. I'm good by myself. To get myself from where I was to where I am now, I had to be."

"So, no husband in your future? Or kids, or the proverbial cottage with the white picket fence?"

"Not necessarily. I'm human. There are a lot of things I want for myself. But I'm also practical. If I don't get them, I'm perfectly fine alone. It works either way."

They stopped at a wooden door with a temporary cardboard sign tacked to it, reading "Dr. Jack Hanson, MD."

"So, you don't date?" he asked her.

"I do, sporadically, if someone is interesting enough. Haven't for a couple of years, though. It was always such an…effort. And I've never cared enough for anyone to get involved in the sense that I wanted to *belong* to him." She shrugged. "I'm not sure what it will take. Not even sure I want to find out."

"Don't you ever get lonely?"

"Don't you?" she countered. "You're not married, and I'm assuming you're not involved."

"Not involved," he said quite simply.

"And you live alone?" The question might have been a leap, but she didn't see Jack living with anybody. He was the epitome of the solitary man and it seemed he worked hard to keep himself isolated.

"Just me. No dogs, cats, or other critters. Prefer to keep my life…uncluttered."

"I'm betting you don't go out with friends too often either."

"Hardly ever."

"So, don't *you* get lonely?" she asked. Passing through the door into his office, he placed his hand in the small of her back as she walked by him, then followed her in. She gritted her teeth against the inevitable shiver. She didn't understand why he got to her that way, but he did. There was no denying that as she shivered and this time he noticed it.

"You OK?" he asked. "It starts getting chilly this time of year. Do you need a sweater or something? I could get you a surgical gown to put on over your clothes, if you want. It might warm you up a little."

What she needed was more of him. More of the shivers he caused. More of the things she'd never allowed herself to want before—the pure carnal need for him. Of course, she was going to keep that to herself and try harder to keep her peculiar reactions to him to herself, as well. Especially since he'd all but told her he didn't want involvement.

"I'm fine. Just acclimating myself to Montana weather, that's all." Yeah, right. More like acclimating herself to the touch of a man who triggered sparks.

A man she didn't even know very well but suddenly had thoughts of in a way she'd never thought of another man. "But thanks for the offer."

"Anyway, no, I'm not lonely," he continued, forging ahead with their conversation. "I keep myself busy. Put in a lot of hours at the hospital. I'm adding some finishing touches to my cabin in my spare time. Helping my buddy Caleb around his place from time to time, since he's still slightly incapacitated. It all adds up to a pretty full day." He closed the office door behind him, then gestured her to the chair in front of his desk. "Oh, and right now I'm trekking up the mountain every day to take care of about a billion cats."

"How is Priscilla, by the way?" Carried asked, wondering if Jack ever did anything for himself. Anything for fun. Even in her own isolation, she'd taken time for her few friends, gone to the gym, occasionally treated herself to a movie. But did he do anything other than what he had to do? It didn't seem so.

"She's doing better than ever. Moving home, against family wishes, the day after tomorrow."

"Everybody has to do what they have to do," Carrie said. "I know how it is. And, for what it's worth, I respect your grandmother for living exactly the way she wants. Not many people have that choice. Too many things get in the way."

"She does live the way she wants. But I worry."

"Which means you're a good grandson." And she liked that, as she'd never seen much devotion in her life, and the devotion for his grandmother she saw in Jack was nice. It gave her hope that someday she might have someone to be that devoted to. Or someone might be that devoted to her. If a distant sort of character like Jack could have it… "Well, if you'd like me to spot you on the cat care, I could go up later today so you could do…whatever it is you do."

"Thanks for the offer, but there's a knack to it. As in dump the food into the bowls, then run like hell before you get fur-balled to death." He chuckled over that.

Carrie laughed, too. Despite the appearance he tried to put on, Jack *was* a caring man. She wasn't sure he knew how to show it. But it was there. She could see it. "Well, if there's anything else I can do—make a few house calls, go to the store and pick up some cat food, go up to see Priscilla from time to time once she's settled back in…"

"I'm good," he said. "Unless you're looking for something to fill your lonely spaces."

"They're not lonely spaces, Jack. I've never had anyone in my life for more than the blink of an eye, so when you don't have it, you don't know what it's about. Consequently, I look at my life more in terms of empty spaces. Not lonely ones. I read, work out, go out with friends occasionally. It suits me."

"Is that denial I'm hearing, or acquiescence?"

"Neither one. It's practicality. Because above all I try to be practical about everything. Had to be that way to survive being tossed from place to place as I was, then eventually ending up on the streets. If you can't be practical about it, you won't make it, and it was always my intention to make it." She smiled. "Anyway, enough about me. You said you wanted to talk to me about something?"

"I did." He crossed over to the cabinet that held his coffee maker, then poured her a cup, offered her cream and sat down across from her. Very deliberately. Very precisely, almost like he measured every movement. Like a man who took control of each and every movement, voluntary as well as involuntary.

It was oddly fascinating, she thought. Almost a glimpse into something she hadn't expected. Jack Hanson was a man who took great care to present himself properly. It mattered to him. He cared about his mark—his spot in time. That revelation didn't cause goose bumps, but it did cause a curiosity over what had turned someone like him away from life in general.

"Well, as it turns out, I wanted to talk about your varied background," he continued, bringing her back into the conversation. "Learn a little more about you other than what you said on your application and what you've told me. I'd like to learn more about the specifics of Carrie Kellem, since they may come into play in your training."

"Seriously? Is *that* why you chose me for your program, because I didn't have a traditional life? Because, somehow, you think that coming from the streets the way I did will make me tougher, or braver? Or hold me back from what I need to do?" She was offended, and didn't try to hide it, as the notion that her varied background was the reason she'd gotten to where she was now didn't wash. It didn't give way to the fact that it wasn't her background that made her tougher or braver, but her desire to put her background behind her.

"I don't like that, Jack. I've worked *hard* to get

away from it, and I don't want it to be the main reason I'm here. It's over. I don't want where I was to be the reason or cause of getting anything. No favors, no special consideration. Nothing. So if I haven't earned my spot rightfully, then I'm out of here, varied background or not." She started to rise from her chair, but he stood up from the desk, leaned over it and laid a gentle hand on her shoulder.

"Your upbringing, or lack of it, isn't why I chose you, Carrie. Your application stated you'd been homeless, but that didn't matter to me. But I do think it's at least, in part, the reason you have the qualifications I want. You know, a character-building thing. Because you're a good medic, and I've seen that in person already. You're enthusiastic to learn. And smart. Also, you don't get beaten down. There's a part of me that envies that because I've been in a rut for a very long time. I don't always find the joy in my job that you find in yours. I still give it my best, but I don't go at it anymore the way I see you go at it. You squeeze the essence out of every opportunity, while I simply let it dribble by.

"But would you have had those qualities if you hadn't had to fight so hard for them? I don't know. And it doesn't matter. But don't deny your background, Carrie. You can hate it, you can fight to overcome it, you can curse it every day of your life. But it's part of who you are. And while I didn't accept you into my program because of where you came from, I did accept you because I believe your struggles have made you an ideal candidate." He shrugged. "So, no offense intended."

"None taken," she conceded. Because he was right. She'd spent a lifetime trying to overcome it, and had never really looked at the trash bins and alley doorways as an education of sorts. But it had been. Still, she didn't have to like it. She would always try to keep it in her past. But now she saw it a little differently.

"I know I'm defensive or apologetic because of where I come from. I suppose it's a habit that, when someone brings it up, I get defensive. Or overreact. But I've been the recipient of a lot of handouts in my life, and I don't want that. I never had stability. Got tossed from foster home to foster home. Nobody wanted to keep me. I couldn't get educated properly as I was in and out of so many schools they lost track of me. And I was out on the street, on my own, when I was sixteen. Picking up aluminum cans and turning them in for money. Doing any odd job someone had for me. Except the sexual ones. *I never did that.*

"But I lived in alleys, Jack. Slept under cardboard boxes or in doorways, rain, shine or snow. People would see me on the street and toss me bits of leftover food from restaurant containers. Food they were taking home to their dogs. And I was grateful for it because it hadn't been in the bottom of the garbage for days, which was what I was used to. They'd also bring me charity clothes that didn't fit, and blankets that should have been tossed away because they were so worn. Handouts—that's all I had for a lot of years. So, when I jumped to the conclusion that my spot here was another handout…" She shrugged. "Didn't mean to come off the way I did. Sorry." She sat back down, managed a repentant smile. "So, again, why am I here?"

"I…I don't know what to say." His voice was

unsteady, his eyes betraying shock and compassion.

"There's nothing *to* say. That was then, this is now. And I'm fighting hard to stay in the now."

"So how did you get from there to here?"

"Saved every penny I could from all the odd jobs I worked. Checked into a shelter where I was given three squares a day, shower facilities and a bed. Took a *practical* look at the things I could do, given my circumstances, then finished my schooling. Met an old cop who told me I ought to consider trying out for the academy, that it could change my life. I did when I was old enough, because I really wasn't headed in any direction and that seemed as good as anything. He was right, too. I got accepted, and that opened the world to me. Taught me things I didn't know. Showed me things I'd never seen. After a while, though, after I was a cop, I started asking myself if this was all there was."

"And the answer was obviously no."

"Which brought me here," she said, smiling. "Lucky me and, hopefully, lucky you."

Jack shook his head. "I didn't know it was that

rough, Carrie," he said. "I can't even respond because I can't picture it. Can't picture *you* in it."

"You don't have to," she said. "Because I'm not in it anymore. I'm here. Starting a new chapter. Another step further away."

"Well, maybe what I have in mind's going to be even another step further." He took a sip of his coffee and turned in his chair to gaze out the window. Seemed to get lost for a few seconds, then blinked himself back into the moment. "I have something in mind for you that won't be easy. Provided you measure up in my program."

"Ah, the story of my life. Another step, maybe a new dream born. So, what is it, Jack? What is this opportunity?"

"The wide-open spaces of Montana. No walls to confine you. No real rules to follow except to do the job the best way you can find. And living by your wits. You, more than anybody I've ever known, could do that. So, care to take a drive with me while I tell you more?"

It was a beautiful autumn day, the temperatures hadn't started dipping too much yet, even though that would happen in the next couple of weeks, and the fresh air was beckoning him. Not to mention the restlessness pushing him to do something different. That was the only reason he was going out there right now, and if he tried hard enough, he might even convince himself of it. Because introducing Carrie to Saka'am could have waited, since she wasn't even in training yet. And he could have asked one of the other part-time doctors or even nurses at Sinclair Hospital to do this. But it had been so long since he'd been there, and he needed to go back, even though he'd vowed, five years ago, he never would. Times changed, so did attitudes. So, while his hadn't moved much toward that in the preceding years, even he couldn't argue himself out of the notion that he had to do this. Had to start facing up to it. Or, at least, try.

But he didn't want to go back alone because he did have to see to the medical needs. And if the memories of Evangeline and Alice brought him down to a point where he couldn't function as he should, he'd have Carrie there to pick up the slack. That, plus the idea of assigning her to

Saka'am eventually. "There's a little community of Native Americans—the Confederated Salish and Kootenai tribes. They don't live on the reservation, even though they're connected to it. Mostly, they're into lumbering, which usually happens sometime between the leaf drop and winter solstice, and right now they're fully engaged in harvesting crops. So this is a busy time of year for them and it's not always convenient for a lot of the people there to get over to the reservation to take care of basic medical needs.

"Years ago, when I wasn't much more than a toddler, my mother and I started going out every few weeks to tend to their medical care. In the fall, it was always about immunizing the children then, of course, seeing to other medical needs. It's that time now, and since Mom and Henry are semiretired, and Caleb and Leanne are away, it's up to me to get it done. So, I thought that since I've got the time right now, I'd head on out there and get the process started, spend the night, finish up tomorrow, then come back home later in the day in time to pick up my shift tomorrow night."

"Which has what to do with me?"

"I want you to go with me. I've checked your schedule, and it seems you're scheduled off until tomorrow night. So, if you're interested, we can leave within the next hour, which means we'll get there midafternoon, work until dark, then begin again tomorrow morning, and finish up midafternoon."

"Which would mean spending the night?" she asked.

"It's too long a drive to come back tonight so, yes, spend the night. Somebody there will take us in."

"You're sure of that?"

"They always have before. They're a very hospitable people. Friendly, generous…" Sometimes too much so.

"The workload?"

"Vaccinations. Physicals. General care, for the most part."

"So, why me, Jack? I mean, I'm excited to do something different. I've never had the opportunity to work in a clinic-type setting, so I want to do this. But why are you asking me and not someone with more experience? I'm a paramedic and usually we don't do general medical care."

"But you're capable, aren't you?"

"Of course, I'm capable. But I'm also curious."

"OK. Saka'am and the surrounding area is fairly well populated. The people are spread out so there's no central core, and I need someone to cover that area on a more regular basis. Also to head up rescue operations in a large geographic area out there. I've made this plan to provide better and closer rescue and basic medical coverage in specific areas and, tentatively, I've matched you to Saka'am because it will be a challenge with the way it's spread out. Also because I have ties there, and I want them to have my best, which I hope will be you."

"I think I'm flattered," she said.

"It's always an uphill battle out here, Carrie. It's a mix between dealing with the traditional Native American ways and what society expects or perceives. These people are just normal folks. They work, they go to school, to church…they dress like we do. Have the needs we do. But it's a struggle for them to hold on to their traditions, and too many outsiders go into these situations expecting to change things…things that don't need changing. Names. Lifestyle. It's important to find someone who can deal with the intermingling of both worlds, and respect the fact that they might resort to a sweat lodge over modern medicine. Because I don't see you as someone who would interfere with what is already established, that's why I want you to cover the area." Also, because he owed the people of Saka'am his best. Which wasn't him. Not anymore. But it could be Carrie.

"I don't know what to say," she said. "No one's ever had that kind of trust in me before."

He wondered if she'd ever had that kind of trust in herself. "Well, it's going to be a lot of responsibility because part of my plan is to give them better access to medical care than they've ever had. But you'll still have to take orders from me. And you cannot, as you called it, jump the scene. I can't put a doctor out there. It's not practical. And I can't even go with a nurse because we have a shortage of them at the hospital. But a paramedic is the perfect person because you're trained in medicine and first response. You don't get to act independently, though. There will be a lot of situations that won't be yours to call. And even though I might not be on-site, I'll still be the one who makes the big decisions. Which does have me concerned. I'll be honest about that."

"I'm not going to mess this up, Jack. It's an opportunity I never expected and…" She swallowed hard, fighting back her emotion. "I mean, I know I've got a long way to go before you turn me loose, but…thank you." She swiped back a tear and sniffled. "Thank you."

He really wanted this to work out. Saka'am needed more than they had, and Carrie needed more, as well. In her vulnerable moments it was so clear. But she fought that vulnerability. Fought it hard. So he was worried about whether this was the right decision, especially since she hadn't even started her training yet. But, well… there was something about Carrie that drew him in more and more every time he saw her. And he couldn't stop himself from reacting. "So, go home, pack an overnight bag, and I'll pick you up in a little while."

Carrie pushed herself out of the chair and smiled. "I'll be waiting." Then she hurried out his door.

And Jack…well, he stayed in his chair a few minutes longer, wondering why he'd just done that. He had all the good reasons ready on the tip of his tongue but there was another one, one he wasn't willing to give serious thought to. That was the one that made him nervous. The unthinkable thought that was beginning to unravel him. The one that made him do something he wouldn't normally do—get involved. And, any way he looked at it, he *was* involved.

"You didn't tell me there weren't any roads out here," she said, holding on to the truck door for dear life.

The road *was* a bumpy one. There was a better way to get to Saka'am, but this *shortcut* shaved off a good thirty minutes. And he was already later than he'd wanted to be. "This is a fine road," he shouted, so she could hear him above the rattling of the truck and the road noises. "It's passable."

"Then what you're telling me is that if the road is passable, it's a good road?"

"Any road that gets me where I'm going is a good road." It was a statement that reflected his life, as he'd never expected to be taking this road again. Not in the literal sense, but in the much broader one where hiding from the realities of his world now seemed the preferable thing to do.

"Are you sure there's a town at the end of it?"

He chuckled. "Last time I was out here there was. It takes some endurance to get there. And we *are* taking the road less traveled."

"The road bound to cause orthopedic injuries?" she asked, rubbing her back.

"Not if you're used to it," he said, swerving to avoid a deep rut in the road and effectively sending Carrie lurching sideways, straight into him, despite her seat belt holding her in place. "You OK?" he asked.

It took her a couple of seconds to push away from him, and in that short span of time he put his arm across her shoulder protectively. Brushed his hand across her cheek as he did so, which caused her to shiver.

And while his touch didn't mean anything to him—he probably wasn't even aware of it—it meant something to her, as the goose bumps sprang immediately to her arms, and her breath caught in a sharp little gasp. Not from the colliding of bodies, though. From the gentle near caress that had come afterward. Her first thought was to linger there another moment or two, to smell the slight hint of lime in his aftershave, or enjoy the hard muscle of his upper arm or the surprising smoothness of the hand that had barely brushed across her cheek. Maybe she was indulging herself in a fantasy…

But that would be obvious, and silly, and there was no point. She wasn't living in a fantasy here. And all the things running through her head for those brief seconds were pure fantasy. Being held. Stroked. Making love. "Ask me in the morning," she said, straightening back up, "when I can, or can't, get out of bed." She looked over into the back seat where Bella was sitting to make sure she was OK. The dog seemed happy to be there, though. And unfazed by the bumpy ride. Even so, she reached back to pat her.

"Then let me prescribe a long, hot shower when we get home tomorrow."

"Not tonight?"

"Oh, the aches and pains won't have set in by then. It usually takes a good twelve hours or so."

"Which means by the time I wake up in the morning..."

"You'll be feeling it. But there won't be much you can do about it because the people there don't have a hot tub like I do."

"Is that an invitation?"

"It is, unless you want to take a long, hot shower in your apartment. *If* you have hot water."

Carrie moaned. "Where I'm living, if you get water doing anything more than dripping from the showerhead, it's a miracle, and lukewarm is a luxury."

"Well, like I said...the hot tub. Plenty of hot water. Nice, massaging jets." He stopped himself before he let it turn into a real invitation complete with a specific time attached to it. *Tomorrow night, my place at seven, hot tub. Clothes optional.* Yeah, like that was what he needed—an image of her in his tub, clothes optional. Hell, what clothes? What red-blooded man would invite a lady to the tub with the option of clothes?

The one who was so out of practice he couldn't even remember the way the man-woman thing worked anymore. Not that he wanted it. But, still, it was there, finally waking up again. At the wrong time, in the wrong place. In a man who'd taken a personal vow, years ago, that he wouldn't travel that path again.

"Depending on how the rest of this trip goes, I might take you up on that offer," Carrie said, adjusting herself in her seat again, thanks to another big chunk of pitted road. "So, do you invite all your paramedics back to your place?"

"Actually, in the few weeks it's been my place, the only person I've invited there, besides you, is Priscilla."

Carrie laughed. "I heard Melanie Clark at the hospital has a big crush on you. Bet she'd accept an invitation."

"If I offered one. Which I won't. Not to her, not to anybody else."

"Except me and your grandmother," Carrie said. "Not sure how to take that, Jack. Are you placing me in the same category as your grandmother? You know, as in cozy friend or relative?"

"Trust me, my grandmother's not anywhere near *your* category." And there was nothing about Carrie he wanted to turn into a cozy friendship.

"Which is?" she asked.

He glanced over at her. Saw her smiling. And the twinkle in her eyes. She was baiting him. Teasing him. Testing him. Maybe even…flirting? No, she wasn't flirting. She couldn't be. Wouldn't be. Except that smile… "Tactical paramedic and professional woman. No-nonsense. Practical."

"Well, now I know why you don't date. I mean, seriously, no-nonsense? Practical? You need to get a better style if you ever intend on inviting a woman to your hot tub for anything other than soaking her achy muscles." She laughed, then turned her attention to the scenery outside, while Jack loosened his grip on the steering wheel and forced himself to concentrate on the road ahead. And *only* on the road, until they reached Saka'am, where he turned onto a dirt road that ran a curious, crooked path to the center of the two-street town. Right past the cemetery he wouldn't look at.

Saka'am was basically an intersection in the middle of nowhere, where one road crossed another, with several buildings standing along each of four directions. Then nothing but houses dotting the general area surrounding it. All the structures were white, wooden clapboard in one shape or another, each had trim of different colors, and all of it looked very tidy, well kept. And almost ghostly.

"So, this is all there is to it? No other houses than what I'm seeing?"

"Most of the houses are spread out. Not too many people live in town. They fish, hunt, farm…and they live where they do that. Pretty much like rural areas everywhere."

"Well, it's certainly not Chicago, is it?"

"And that's a bad thing?" he asked, as he brought his truck to a stop in front of the church, and twisted in his seat to wave at the line of people beginning to form at the door.

Victor Redbone, the town grocer and owner of the one and only restaurant in Saka'am, a diner that served early breakfast, then closed for the day, was already jotting names on a yellow legal pad. And Chief Charley Begay, an old-time fixture who was highly regarded as the self-appointed leader of the community, scowled at everyone heading toward the town hall, eager to get their names on the medical list. There were many familiar faces Jack was glad to see. And his father-in-law, Chief Charley, a face he didn't want to see.

Carrie laughed as she hopped out of the vehicle. "I'll let you know later," she said, as a wave of eager, laughing women swept her straight inside the building.

Jack watched her disappear, then sighed. It was probably a mistake dragging her into a part of his world he kept hidden. But she caught him up and engaged him in ways that even Evangeline hadn't been able to do. Of course, what kind of husband had he been to Evangeline? The worst. The very worst. So it wasn't fair to compare.

Still, with Carrie…

CHAPTER FOUR

"JUST THOUGHT YOU'D like to know, your dog is heading off south," Jack said, tossing his backpack down on a table set up in the community meeting room, as several of the locals scurried about, arranging chairs, setting out pitchers of water, and doing whatever else they thought would be helpful. He looked for Palloton among them, saw him standing at the front door. Observing him. Then Carrie. Assessing the situation as only Palloton would do. Palloton, his best friend. The only friend he'd kept after—

Carrie, who was standing at the table, already setting up to give immunizations, spun around to face him. "She won't go far. She likes to get the lay of the land when we go someplace new."

"Well, all I'm saying is…wolves. They don't wander into town this time of the day, usually, but they're out there, and unless your dog—"

"Bella," Carrie interrupted.

"Unless *your dog* is experienced in this kind of location, I'd suggest you secure her before she wanders too far or gets herself into the kind of trouble only a city dog could get into."

"Am I sensing a double meaning there?" she asked him.

"It's a broad warning. People, *or dogs*, come out here expecting one thing, and end up with something entirely different. Sometimes good, sometimes bad." In his life, he'd had both. One had made him soar with the eagles—invincible. The other had hurt him more than he'd known a person could hurt. "All I'm saying is, if you want to make sure you leave here with your dog tomorrow, you should take better care of her today." Bitter words. Words that felt like acid on his tongue. Words he wished someone had pounded into him all those years ago when he hadn't taken care of Evangeline.

Jack drew in a deep breath, then let it out slowly. "Anyway, I think we're going to have a few more people coming in than I'd expected. A lot of them want to see me, and, according to

Victor, they haven't been getting regular medical care lately. Too busy to go to the reservation, and it's a long trip over there. So, unless it's absolutely necessary, lots of things go unattended. Like health matters."

"I can't imagine that. Even when I was homeless, there was always a clinic… I really am a city girl, aren't I?"

"Through and through." Which wasn't a bad thing to be. But he liked this place better. He'd hated his years in Phoenix, had always wanted to come home. He'd tried several times. Once, he'd even gotten as far as the Montana border, then had turned around and gone right back to his city life. And hated it all over again. He didn't belong there. It was a beautiful city, as cities went. But too loud. Too many cars. Too much congestion. And now…well, now he was back where his heart had always told him he belonged. But could he stay? *Would* he stay?

That was always the question, and being back in Saka'am wasn't the answer. Unfortunately, he didn't know what was.

"Anyway…" He finally gave way to a forced

smile—a smile he put on for the sake of the people waiting in line to see him. Because nothing inside him wanted to smile. "I suppose it's time to get to work. People are waiting. So, go find that dog—"

"Bella," she interrupted.

"That dog," he countered. "Get her back here and we'll open up to patients." He still didn't want to go through with this, still didn't want to dredge up the memories and face the people who'd been here, the people who'd seen, who still knew. But doing it with Carrie at his side made it better. Did he deserve that, though? Probably not. But he was grateful for it anyway.

"Wiwa," Palloton said, finally approaching Jack. "It's been a while."

Jack turned to face his onetime best friend. "Too long," he said, giving himself over to the embrace as Palloton offered it. An embrace with the person he'd once considered his brother. "You're looking good." It had been months since he'd seen Palloton face-to-face. A quick trip to Phoenix, a night to reminisce. They'd kept in touch shortly after the tragedy, but times changed, Palloton had got married, they'd grown apart. So their relationship had turned into emails, texting, occasional phone calls, less than occasional face time on a computer. And the odd infrequent visit when Palloton came to see him.

"Married life does that to you," he said, smiling. Palloton was tall, well muscled, with long black hair flowing freely down to the middle of his back. He pulled it back into a neat ponytail on the days he donned a suit to be a lawyer, and on the other days he opted for jeans, T-shirt and boots, much the way everyone else dressed in Saka'am. Today, Palloton was casual. "I'd heard you were going to be the one coming out here and it…surprised me."

"Surprised me, too," Jack replied. "Thought about sending someone else, but…" He shrugged. Someone else couldn't have done what he needed to do here…to figure out how to face his past. Not to put it away, not to start a whole new life, but to face the old one.

"Well, it's about time you came to me. I'm the

one who's dragged myself down to Phoenix to see you, and it's your turn to reciprocate."

"Trust me, this isn't about reciprocating anything."

Palloton looked over at Carrie, who was busy counting doses of vaccinations. "Because of her?" he asked, his voice lowered so only Jack could hear him.

Jack glanced across the room at Carrie, too. She was gorgeous, in such an unassuming way. He'd bet she didn't even know it, which made her even more gorgeous. He was attracted to her. No denying that. But that was all he'd allow himself. A look. A moment to admire. Nothing else. "No. I'm not…ready for that. Don't know if I ever will be. She just happened to be the one most available to come with me." He didn't have to tell Palloton that he'd switched his own schedule to match hers, hoping they could do this together.

"You don't deserve to spend the rest of your life alone, Wiwa. You're paying a penance you don't need to pay."

Jack, who was still focused on Carrie, shook his head. "I'm paying what I have to pay." He looked back at Palloton. "I can't control it. It's what I have to do."

"That's not a good way to live, my friend. Especially when you've got someone like her on your side." He looked over at Carrie another time, then shook his head. "You're missing out."

"My choice." Jack sighed heavily. "My life, my decision."

"But are you happy with it?"

Jack regarded Carrie once more before he began to work. He didn't answer Palloton. What was there to say? Happiness wasn't part of him anymore. Stray glances from afar, an infrequent wish, but not true happiness.

After pulling several medicine vials from his pack, Jack carried them across the room to Carrie, who was trying to be unobtrusive in a room full of strangers, but not doing a very good job of it as most of the eyes in the room were on her. Everybody was probably wondering if she was the one who had replaced Evangeline. Speculations, maybe some good wishes for him. And memories. Lots of memories as everyone had loved Evangeline. She would have been here with him today, helping him set up. Organizing the queue the way Victor and Palloton were now doing. Jack was sure there were many people lining up outside who were thinking the same things. "You ready to get started?" he asked her.

"Yep," she said, cheerfully. "As soon as I go get Bella. So, the guy you were talking to…"

"Best friend," Jack said, without embellishment.

"He's working with us today? Is he a medic?"

"Nope. He's an attorney. Great climber. True advocate for the tribe. And from the looks of it, he's setting up to handle the mobs."

"Mobs, really?" Carrie's eyes went wide in amazement.

Regardless of his glum mood, Jack laughed. Carrie was so cute…that expression of surprise on her face. The look of anticipation. She was eager to do this. Probably considered it another move forward. He liked her enthusiasm. Liked the way she just went at life with everything she had. Wished he could have some of that in himself. "Little mobs. Polite ones. Friendly ones. They'll bring cookies and fry bread."

"Back in Chicago, the word mob has a different connotation. And, trust me, *those* mobs didn't bring cookies."

"Then, aren't you glad you're here, and not in Chicago?" He was. He truly was. "So, let me introduce you to Palloton, since he's the one who'll be sending the patients through."

"Not only sending them through but sorting the gifts they bring." Palloton pointed to the several plates of cookies, the different varieties of autumn squash, the sacks of fresh-picked apples already filling up the table next to the door. "In Saka'am, even though grants through the reservation cover our medical costs, we like to pay back." He extended his hand to Carrie. "I'm Palloton Yellowfeather, by the way. Wiwa's oldest and, I hope, best friend."

"Why do you call him Wiwa? Does that have significance?"

"It's Salish, for wild," Jack explained. "It was the nickname they gave me when my mother would bring me out here with her and turn me loose on the community when she was working. I wasn't…"

"He wasn't the best-behaved kid in town," Palloton said, laughing. "Which is why all the other kids liked him. He got away with the things we couldn't."

"Such as?" Carrie asked, looking back and forth between the men.

"Sneaking off to go fishing or climbing when we were supposed to be attending to chores. My mother would tell us to mow the yard or weed her vegetable garden, and the next thing you knew, we'd be scaling a rock or rafting down a river. For Wiwa, there was always something else to do. Something fun. And being the impressionable child I was…"

"Whoa," Jack said. "You were never impressionable. *Never.* In fact, when your mom told us to do something…" He glanced over at Carrie. "I was here all the time. Even when my mom wasn't working. So I was treated as one of the locals. Assigned chores, given responsibilities suited to my age. Anyway, as I recall, every time your mom had something for us to do, you were the one who expected me to come up with a way to, let's just call it, *circumvent* it."

Carrie laughed. "So, Palloton, you were the instigator and Jack the enabler?"

"Something like that," Palloton replied, as the first patient stepped through the door. An older man, who handed Jack a knit cap.

"Beautiful work," Jack said, showing the man back to his examining area. "I still have that sweater Rayne knit me all those years ago."

"She keeps you in her heart, Jack. Even though you're not here, she pays tribute to both of them when she can."

"His wife and daughter," Palloton explained, once Jack was gone. "Rayne was Evangeline's teacher in school. Would have been Alice's, too, if she'd…" He swallowed hard. Didn't finish what he was saying.

"Jack was married?" she asked. Somehow, this shocked her, even after what Priscilla had hinted at.

"He didn't tell you?" Palloton said, then immediately backed off.

"Not a word. But we don't have the kind of relationship where he would." Still, she wondered why he hadn't mentioned it. Divorce was tragic, but nothing to be ashamed of. Had it been a bad marriage—the kind that, once you were out of it, you put it out of your mind? Had the end of it been her fault or his? And what about his daughter? Had his ex-wife taken her away? Was that why Jack was always so glum—because he didn't get to see his little girl?

There were so many questions she wanted to know answers to but they were questions she had no right to ask. Especially since Jack had chosen not to tell her about this part of his life.

"Well, I suppose he'll tell you all about it in good time," Palloton said, turning his attention to the computer in front of him, obviously embarrassed that he'd given away something Jack didn't want given away. "In the meantime," he went on, still focusing on his computer screen, "are you a doctor, nurse or what? I need to know so I can record it in the charts."

"Paramedic. All properly certified."

"And you've moved to Marrell to…?" He glanced up at her then smiled. "Personal question, not legal. Just trying to make dull conversation after inserting my foot in my mouth."

Carrie laughed. "I'm taking Jack's rescue course at the hospital. Looking for some new direction in my life."

"Well, I'm glad you were directed here, Carrie Kellem. Jack seems happier than he's been in a while."

"It's the class," she said, uncomfortable with the direction this conversation was going. "Not me."

"Well, whatever it is, it's good to have him back home, where he belongs." This time Palloton turned his undivided attention to the computer screen, while Carrie went outside to find Bella.

"She doesn't know," Jack said, stepping up to Palloton. "At least, she didn't until you told her."

"Shouldn't she have?"

"It's not that kind of relationship."

"I saw the way you were looking at her, Wiwa. All I can say is maybe it should be."

"Not open for discussion," Jack said.

"Is Charley open for discussion? Because he didn't look too pleased to see you. Did he know you were coming?"

Jack shook his head. "And it wasn't my intention to tell him. But he saw me coming in, so I suppose *that* cat is out of the bag, too."

"Not good form, Jack. He has a right—"

"It's got nothing to do with him," Jack interrupted.

"He was Evangeline's father and Alice's grandfather, and he blamed you for their deaths. He suffers for it the way you do, which makes it everything to do with him."

"And I didn't blame myself? That's all I've been doing for five years. So he can blame me all he wants. He's welcome to do it. I deserve it."

"Tell yourself whatever you want, but you've got to put *all* the pieces back together before you can move on. A little bit here and a little bit there won't cut it. And Charley's one of those pieces."

"Who says I want to move on?" Jack questioned, trying to hold back the anger that wanted to flare in him. He wasn't mad at Palloton, though. He was mad at himself. For so many things.

"You do, every time you look at Carrie. Whether she's the one, I don't know. But she's the start of it, my friend. So, as they say, it's time to wake up and smell the coffee."

Maybe Palloton was right. But suddenly Jack didn't have the same fondness for coffee he'd had only moments earlier. In fact, even the thought of it made his stomach churn.

From just down the hall, Carrie heard the conversation between Jack and Palloton. She hadn't intended to, but when her name had come up, she'd stopped and listened. Not only had Jack been married, he'd had a daughter. She had no idea how they'd been killed but Jack blamed himself for it, which explained so much about his demeanor. Her heart went out to him. It was all connected to Saka'am somehow, and she knew it couldn't be easy on him, coming back here. She was curious to know more, but it was Jack's life and his memories. There were parts of herself she didn't divulge, and she understood that in him. Better than most.

So, rather than staying around, hoping to hear more, she headed out and passed by Chief Charley, whom she now knew was Jack's father-in-law. She smiled at him, but his response was a scowl. Which she understood, since she was connected to Jack and, thus, the chief's sentiments toward Jack. But she felt sorry for the man. He'd lost so much—a daughter, a granddaughter, a son-in-law. Such deep sadness. Another thing she understood.

Bella hadn't gone too far by the time Carrie caught up to her. Just a couple of short blocks. And as she hiked the main street to grab her dog, people smiled at her, gave her friendly waves. One woman greeted her with a basket of muffins. She could see why Jack had always been drawn to this place. Why he always returned. It was so sad now that Saka'am held bad memories.

Well, it wasn't her concern, was it? Securing Bella and getting to work was, however. So, she tied the leash to her dog and headed back to the church, passing Chief Charley again on the way. Decked in baggy jeans and a white cotton shirt, he wore a cowboy hat with a feather sticking out of it. His typical long, black hair was streaked with gray and pulled back in a braid. And as for his dark, angry eyes… No, it wasn't anger she saw there. It was sadness. The same sadness she caught glimpses of in Jack. In a life where she struggled so hard to get over her own sadness, she wondered if some sadness couldn't be overcome. She'd always thought it could be, or hoped so, but now she wasn't sure because, for some reason, she could feel the sadness in her. And it wasn't her sadness she was feeling.

The stream of patients had been steady for the first three hours. Without a break. Mostly minor complaints…arthritis aches and pains, stomach problems, worries that didn't amount to much. Each time he'd stepped outside his little area, he'd noted the children being escorted back to Carrie. Palloton had said she was good with them, that she had a natural way.

He'd also mentioned she was doing cursory physicals on each of them who came through, patching cuts and scratches, doing other medical procedures she was qualified to do. Jack was glad for that, glad she was taking the initiative because that was what all these little outlying communities needed—medical initiative. Someone to take control and fix the problems as they presented themselves. Not wait until someone showed up to take care of matters when it was convenient, the way it had always been.

He held out a lot of hope that Carrie would be that person as he cared so much for Saka'am he didn't want to turn the medical care over to just anyone. Of course, that meant he wouldn't see her too often. Which didn't sit as well with him as he'd hoped it would. He liked seeing her. Liked catching the occasional glimpse. Especially liked working with her, having that contact. Liked being caught up in something different and fun and with so much potential, even if only for small snatches of time.

Would he get used to that? He could. Easily. Which was *not* his intention. But Carrie was… infectious. And he didn't mind being a little infected. Just a little, though, because she could turn into a habit. Someone to take up the empty spaces while he was trying to justify it as strictly professional. Someone to count on when he was not used to counting on anyone but himself. Which meant he had to keep this strictly on the professional up-and-up. Quit catching those glimpses. Quit admiring…well, everything but her skills.

Stop it, he said to himself, snapping on gloves in preparation for his next patient—Winona White Horse. He suspected diabetes, and needed to take some blood samples. "What I like to tell my patients is that this isn't going to hurt," he said, as he pushed through the curtain to the makeshift exam, trying to drag a bit of courage with him. Winona had been Evangeline's best friend. Her maid of honor at their wedding. She'd stepped in to help Priscilla, who had acted as midwife when Alice was born, and had held his hand through both funerals. "But it does," he said, forcing a laugh, as the sad memories bombarded him.

"I've missed you," she said, holding out her left arm for him, then watching as he tied the blue rubber tourniquet around it.

"Been busy."

"When I heard you were moving to Marrell, I wondered if you would make it out here, or send us off to the reservation for medical care.

I know it's not easy for you, coming back. But I'm glad you have, because this is your home. Where you belong."

He palpated for a vein, found it, then swabbed the area with an alcohol wipe, hoping the bead of nervous sweat forming on his forehead didn't drop down and contaminate the area. "It goes with the job," he said, deliberately holding back from the vein stick now that his hands were shaking. "That's all."

Winona laid her hand over his to stop the shaking. "Look, Jack. Nobody but the chief ever says anything about it. Nobody blames you. Things were different then. Different lives, different priorities. And you were in a tough spot…we were taking too much from you. We'd never had regular care before, and we were taking advantage of you. Expecting house calls all hours of the day or night. Asking you to drive out to places you shouldn't have had to drive to in order to see a patient who could as easily have come in to you. We were greedy, and you were too good. It all contributed."

He blew out a frustrated breath and backed

away from the exam table. "I contributed," he said quite simply. "Just me. I knew what the job would be like here, and I accepted that. Accepted the fact that some things would be neglected in order to see to others. And I blame myself for that. For…everything."

"I know you do. Everybody knows. But why does everything have to come with blame? What happened was an accident…a horrible tragedy. Nobody, including you, meant it to happen. And after the initial shock of their deaths, nobody blamed you. But you were already gone by then, and probably didn't even know that."

"Palloton told me. But it didn't matter."

"You could have come back, you know."

"To what? I didn't have anything here. No wife, no daughter. Just memories I didn't want to have." He laid down the syringe with which he'd intended to stick her. "Look, I'm going to ask Carrie to draw your blood. You know what they say—doctors are the worst at it. Lucky for you, she's not a doctor."

"I wanted to ask you over for dinner. You've never seen my son, and since you and Palloton and my husband were such good friends, I thought it would be nice for everybody to get together. But Palloton said you'd probably refuse. So, will you…refuse?"

He blinked, then looked her straight in the eyes. "You know why I have to."

"No, I don't, Jack. We're your friends. We have been for a long, long time."

"Except we're not all here anymore, are we?" he said bitterly.

Winona slid off the table but made no effort to leave the area. "We miss her, Jack. We all do. And Alice. But we miss you, too, because even though you're not one of us, you're part of us. Anyway, since I know how stubborn you can get, Palloton asked me to make arrangements for Howard Lone Bear and his family to feed you tonight. And Jane Yazzie has made up her parents' house for you…they're staying on the reservation right now until Ivy delivers. She's having twins, in case you're interested."

"Thanks," he said, sounding not wholeheartedly enthused. He'd known this would be hard, but he hadn't counted on how hard it would be.

In fact, now he wished he'd simply sent Carrie. "Tell William that if he doesn't make it in today, I'll look him up tomorrow."

"He'd like that. You know, he kept that picture of the three of you, the one where you're getting ready to go up the side of Bald Face. That was a good day, Jack. William still talks about it. He wishes the three of you could do it again. Do you still climb?"

"Not lately, but I'm going to…" He shook his head, squeezed his eyes shut and rubbed his forehead. "My mother asked me to teach a mountain rescue course, and climbing goes with it."

"That's what you always wanted, isn't it?"

He nodded.

"Well, I'm glad it's working out for you. Tell Doc Dora for me that we're all behind her in this. William doesn't have time to take the course now, but I'll bet he'd be interested in taking it eventually, if you offer it again, since he's agreed to head up the volunteer firefighters here shortly. Talk to him and see what he thinks."

"I will," Jack said, wondering how he'd ever face someone so tied to his past on a day-today basis, if William did end up taking one of his courses. He was Evangeline's cousin. They'd been raised together as brother and sister. Another one of those bits and pieces Palloton said he needed to resolve. "Whenever he wants to take it, it's on me. No fee. Just let me know when he wants and I'll put him on the roster. Now, let me go up front and tell Carrie what labs to draw on you."

Winona stepped up to Jack, stood on her toes and gave him a kiss on the cheek. "I wish this was better for you Jack," she said sympathetically. "We all do."

He did, too. But the memories, the pain…

How could it not be difficult returning to the place where he'd killed his wife and daughter?

CHAPTER FIVE

THE DAY HAD turned out well. She'd seen all the children on her list, given vaccinations, done checkups, sent a couple of them in to see Jack when she'd suspected conditions that warranted medication—antibiotics for a bronchial infection and an inhaler for asthma. He'd concurred with her diagnoses, which made her feel good, as in her other position as a tactical paramedic her duty was to see and treat immediate concerns, react on the spot, patch them up, then send them along for someone else to diagnose.

Today she had diagnosed, and because she'd got it right, she was feeling pretty good about herself tonight. Jack hadn't mentioned it, though, which disappointed her as she wanted to impress him. Wanted him to see what she could do. Why? She didn't know. Didn't want to think about the implications of what it might be other than an employee trying to impress her boss. That didn't explain the letdown she was feeling, though. But the thought that he might be becoming more important to her than she'd realized did. And left her confused.

But he hadn't said a word, so none of that mattered. Except the idea that her feelings for him could be changing. And that mattered a lot. "So, where are we staying?" she asked lazily, as she and Jack walked side by side down the main road of town, while Bella trailed after them, not particularly interested in anything going on around her since her belly was as full as Carrie's and, like her owner, all she probably wanted to do was settle down somewhere for a good night's sleep.

The lights in the store windows were dim now, and the village had all but gone to bed. Porch lights were blinking off, people who'd been milling around when they'd come down the street earlier had now gone inside. It was so…peaceful. Peaceful like nothing she'd ever known before. And it made her feel good. Like all was right in her world, even if only for that one moment in time.

Instinctively, Carrie slipped her hand into Jack's, not intending a romantic gesture as much as a friendly one. But as her skin slid across his, she felt the tingle pass through her. She wondered if he felt it, too. Wondered if he felt anything at all, ever. Because every time he got to a place where she thought she was going to catch a peek of something beyond what he put on for show, he drew back. Retreated. Doubled his efforts to be the Jack who kept his detachment on display. Like now. She was sure he was trying to find a way to let go of her hand without making a big deal of it.

Surprisingly, after several seconds, Jack didn't pull away. In fact, he grasped her hand a little tighter than she'd expected. Pulled her a little closer into him than she'd anticipated. Yet didn't speak. No, he simply walked alongside her until they reached their appointed lodging for the night, and before they walked up the wooden steps to go inside, he turned to face her.

"We can't do this," he said.

"What? Spend the night in the same house?"

"No. Get involved other than as teacher and

student. I don't do romance, Carrie. I can be your friend, and I'd *like* to be your friend, but that's as far as I can go." Finally, he did let go of her hand. "Everything else—it doesn't work out for me. I'm no good at it."

"Don't you ever hope that someday you might find love or romance or even a commitment? Something that allows someone else in?"

"No. I don't."

"That's a sad way to live, Jack."

"But it's my choice, because it's the only way I can get through my day. It's easier being alone. No complications. No one to hurt. No one to hurt you."

"I know what it's like to be alone. I've spent my entire life there, probably avoiding many of the same things you avoid. And, yes, I do tell people I don't do friendship or even romance because the thought of that kind of commitment scares me. You had a family once…"

He stiffened, pulled away from her. But she reached over and laid a reassuring hand on his arm. "Palloton told me. No details, but I know you've had that kind of love in your life. That kind of commitment. I haven't, and I know, better than anyone, that I put on the front that I don't want it. That's because I don't know what it is. I have no idea how to find a place for it yet. And I say *yet* because I want someone in my life, and I want to reconcile all these things in me that keep me pulled away, because I'd love to be in love. Or have the friend you have in Palloton. Or someone like Priscilla.

"Being alone really is the thing that will hurt you the most, Jack. It's something I know better than you, because you have people around you who do care. I never have, and I know that pain. You don't deserve it, no matter how much you think you do." Carrie stood on tiptoe and brushed a light kiss to his cheek, even though she knew he wouldn't want it. But she did. It felt right, and in her world if it felt right, she went with it. That came of a world that, for a long time, had never felt anything but wrong. A world she didn't want back but that always loomed over her as a threat, telling her how close it really was. "I don't know what your demons are, but I hope you don't let them win."

"They already have," he said sadly as he headed up the steps, alone. But halfway there he stopped, turned around and went back to her. "What I did, Carrie…" He paused, shook his head. "I was the one who caused the loneliness. For my wife. My daughter. I saw what it did to them. Saw what I did to them. So, now that they're gone…why would I deserve any better?"

"We all do things we're not proud of. Things that hurt others. Or ourselves. We all have our lists, but what we do with those lists—" she reached up and brushed her hand across his cheek "—can make us better or destroy us."

"What makes you so wise?" he asked, catching her hand as it brushed his cheek and simply holding it there.

"I could say I've been there, done that. But that makes light of something that causes a lot of pain. What I know, I know from experience. But no matter what, I've always chosen to move on, because if I didn't I'd have spent my life stuck in a place I didn't want to be."

"But have you ever known where you wanted to be?"

"In an idealistic sense, maybe. In reality, I'm working on it. You know, a work in progress." She started to pull her hand from his, but he didn't let go.

"You're doing things to me, Carrie Kellem."

"Even though you just told me we can't do this?" She smiled. His touch, the night air, the stars, the distant howling of a wolf…so perfect. Was this romantic? She didn't know. But it didn't matter because in her narrow world this was the way she had pictured it. Wanted it.

"Did I say that?" he asked as he pulled her into his arms.

"Someone did," she mumbled as he lowered his head and his lips pressed to hers.

His kiss was gentle at first. Then harder. More demanding. The kiss of a starving man, and she responded to it, and kissed him back every bit as hard as he kissed her, because she too was starving. Twining her hands around his neck, she pulled him closer, wanted to feel more of him. Every inch of him pressed to her. Instantly igniting her in ways she'd never been ignited before. In ways that totally shocked her. She'd never felt need like this. Or desire. Or the pure, raw pounding of want. Hadn't known it existed. Didn't know what to do with it other than what she was doing. Kissing him back. Enjoying the sensation of his hands skimming her body, her back, her hips. Enjoying the arousal she could feel pressing her pelvis.

She would have taken more, much more—everything he offered, in fact—his kisses, his passion, his body. And returned the same. But all too soon he broke away from her, stepped back and simply stared at her.

"I suppose I should apologize for that," he finally said. "It wasn't appropriate."

"I know. Because we can't do this," she said, running her fingertips lightly over her already swollen lips, trying to push back the throb of emptiness, the torture of unfulfilled expectations. The letdown that went somewhere far beyond her physical frustrations.

"No, we can't."

But they had. And while he might be denying it to himself, he knew he wanted it. Maybe not in the permanent sense, like happily-ever-after.

She wasn't even sure she believed in that. But for the moment it was good, since that was the way she'd always lived. Moments added up, though. And maybe, just maybe, they might have more moments to add. She hoped so. Because she felt safe with Jack. He wasn't demanding anything. Wasn't taking anything. And that was something new to her. "Do you ever give in and let the *real* Jack Hanson come out? The one who enjoyed our kiss and accepts it for what it was—a nice moment between two people who aren't set on making it out to be anything else?"

"A kiss between friends?"

"Something like that."

He shook his head. "We live in different worlds, Carrie. In mine, *friends* don't kiss like that. And that's the problem because we did, and we can't." That said, he bounded up the steps and into the house, slamming shut the screen door behind him.

Carrie didn't follow him in right away, however. Instead, she stood on the porch, smiling. Then whispered into the night, "Yes, we can. Because we just did."

* * *

Jack was standing in the hall when Carrie finally went inside. He was outside the bedroom doors looking…normal. Looking like he hadn't almost ravaged her on the steps outside. How could he be so cool when her lips still ached? How could he switch himself off so quickly when her pulse was still erratic?

Because he was Jack, and Jack was a master at controlling his switch. Well, most of the time. And that little bit of insight gave her hope. Not for a long-term relationship or something deep and meaningful as much as the glimmer of a better prospect for her future. With Jack? Probably not. And while having something more with him might be nice—the two of them, working side by side, loving each other, taking care of each other…

No, she wouldn't go that far because she doubted Jack would. But she would go far enough to admit that she really didn't want to be alone. That she wanted the things everybody else did. Happiness, love, that special person. She'd denied it in various ways for a long time, but seeing Jack in that same denial made her realize that wasn't who she wanted to be. And for now she did have that little spark of hope that she wouldn't turn out that way.

She feared for Jack, though. His denial was bigger, tougher. All-consuming. And that made her sad.

"Two bedrooms down the hall," Jack said, looking down at Bella, who'd wandered in and found her spot, then plopped down right on his feet. "The larger one should be on the left, the smaller on the right. Bathroom's at the end of the hall."

He wasn't complaining about Bella? That was odd. And his words were rushed. Coming faster and faster. She could hear the breathiness as he spoke. Sense the tension. And…regret? Did he regret not taking her when she'd so obviously been willing to be taken? Or did he regret that he'd come so close? *Had he actually felt something?*

"Jack, we need to—"

"Choose whichever bedroom you want," he

interrupted. "Make yourself comfortable while I run back to the car, grab our bags…"

He was almost choking on his words now, and she could see his panic. See his frantic need to get out of there. All over an intimacy that hadn't happened? What was wrong with him? *What was wrong with her that his regrets were so harsh and immediate?* "Are you OK?" she asked. "Can I do something for you?" He looked on the verge of a panic attack. "Get you a drink of water maybe?" Or were his demons nipping too close to his heels right now?

He shook his head. Drew in a ragged breath. "I'm good. Be right back."

With that, Jack literally ran out the door, and didn't stop running until he was all the way down to the road. She watched him. Saw him stop and simply stand there, like he didn't know what do. Silhouetted against a yellow porch light, she saw his shoulders slump. Saw him drop his head into his hands. Saw him drop to his knees and stay there. Not moving. Saw the way his shoulders moved up and down. Heavy breathing. Or sobbing.

This was a man in trouble and she wanted to go to him, to help. Not as someone trained to respond but as a friend. Only she couldn't. Something stopped her. Stopped her from moving. Or even watching. He wouldn't want that, and he'd probably shut her out, which was what he was good at doing. Shutting people out. Shutting *her* out. So she closed her eyes to Jack, then turned away from the open door. Whatever he was going through, whatever he was feeling or experiencing, he hadn't given her the right to be privy to it. Not even the right to watch it. In fact, just seeing what she'd seen made her feel like she'd betrayed his trust. She didn't understand why or how. But what she did understand was that Jack didn't want to include her. And that hurt because she wanted to be included.

"Well, girl," she said to Bella, who was stretched out on her side on an oval-shaped rag rug, thumping her tail on the floor, "how about we go find out which bed is the most comfortable?"

Taking one final look out the door, she could see Jack was still on his knees. It killed her to turn her back on him—on his suffering. She did, though. And brushed away a tear sliding down her cheek as she did so. A tear shed for something she didn't understand. And something she did.

Jack glanced up at the moon and sighed. He had to go in there. No, this wasn't his home, but it was identical to the house where he and Evangeline and Alice had lived for the year they'd come back to Saka'am. Built by the same builder at the same time, and just like half the houses up and down the road. He hadn't counted on it hitting him so hard when he'd walked in the door, hadn't counted on the way he'd felt after he'd kissed Carrie either. Like something was trying to be reborn. Something he didn't want to let out. Then one step inside, one memory of his own home there, and it had all slammed him down. Almost to the point where he couldn't breathe. So many reminders…

Then there was Carrie. A different kind of reminder. He was attracted to her. More than he wanted to admit. In another place, another lifetime he would have responded to her in a heartbeat. Even this evening he'd thought about it. To put everything out of his head for a little while and take what she was offering. He was a man after all. A man with needs that hadn't surfaced in a long, long time. But that wouldn't be fair to her.

Yes, she wanted him. *He wanted her.* Maybe it was simply physical, maybe more. He didn't want to explore that. Didn't want answers to anything. To take the step that would make him want to find out…who knew what would happen on the other side of it? More guilt to consume him? More memories of what he'd lacked with Evangeline? No, Carrie didn't deserve that.

He did. And that was the point. He deserved the suffering, the misery, the denials. He lived quite well with it now, because the alternative was ugly. Getting back into life? Maybe into a relationship? He knew the final page of that story, and he wasn't willing to drag anybody else onto that page with him. He'd had his shot—loving wife, beautiful daughter. But he'd made other choices. Now he had to live with those choices.

That was the only way he could see his life going forward. The only way he wanted his life to go forward.

But Carrie…damn— Why her? Why now? And why didn't he want to let her into the ugliest part of himself? It was simple, really. He didn't want her to see that side of him. The ugly side that had been the cause of his family's death. He wanted her to think better of him… "Better," he said bitterly. Did he think how he'd just rejected her would make her think better of him? He wasn't worthy of anything better. Didn't want it either. Yet Carrie came so close to making him want it that it scared him. "Carrie Anne Kellem, what are you doing to me?" he asked, as he approached the front door. "What the hell are you doing to me?"

She was making him face himself. That was what. And she didn't even know it. Wouldn't know it either, because he was going to put himself back in order, to sort what he knew he deserved from these feelings creeping in, and put everything where it belonged. Easier said than done, but since when did he merit easy?

* * *

Pushing open the front door, Jack stepped inside the Yazzie house, drew in a deep breath, and braced himself for that short walk down the hall. The lights were out, except for the one in the kitchen, which cast enough of a glow down the hall that he didn't need to turn on another light by which to see. Besides, he had the layout of this house memorized. So he padded quietly, not sure which bedroom Carrie had chosen. He peeked in the first bedroom, the smaller one, and discerned the outline of her in the bed. Ever so quietly, he placed her backpack inside the door, backed away and proceeded on to the next bedroom, where he crept in, lights off, pulled off his shirt, dropped his jeans to the floor, and eased himself into bed. He heaved a sigh of relief when he raised his feet off the floor and lay back. He was glad he hadn't awakened her because it meant no explanations for now, and he'd let the morning take care of itself.

But as he rolled onto his left side, his normal sleeping position, he was greeted with a scream, what seemed like a dozen flailing arms, then an attack from the rear. All in the span of about two seconds. Then the light came on, and he saw Carrie standing on the floor on the other side of the bed, clutching the blanket around her, while her damned dog pinned him flat on the mattress. Licking him in the face.

"What are you doing?" she yelled, backing away until her back was pressed to the wall.

"Get the dog off me," he yelled.

"Why were you in bed with me? Did you think that we— After you pulled away from that kiss, did you really think that you could just come back in here—" she glanced at the clock on the bedside table "—three hours later and pick up where we left off? You turned me down, Jack. I was willing to do something I don't do, and you made it quite clear you weren't interested when I was. Then when you decide you *are* interested…" She shook her head. "Just leave. I don't want to deal with this."

"Get the dog off me," he yelled again, trying to push Bella away. But Bella thought it was playtime, and wrestled him back. "Carrie, I swear, if you don't get this dog…"

Jack managed to roll out from under Bella, which landed him in the middle of the bed, even closer to Carrie, who took a couple of sideways steps, trying to get away from him. "Look, Jack, I don't know what you were expecting here, but when someone turns me down, I walk away from it. Put it in my past."

"Right. You move on. I get that. You've made it perfectly clear," he said, still wrestling with Bella. "But I wasn't expecting *anything*. I thought you were in the other room. I looked in. I saw you there." Or, at least, what he'd thought was her. Or… "Damned dog. She sleeps in a bed, doesn't she?"

A smile began to spread across Carrie's face, and she started to relax. "Most of the time. Usually, she snuggles in with me, so I don't know why she went in there." She giggled. "Maybe she was waiting for you. She does like you, you know."

"I don't care what she likes," he grumbled, suddenly realizing he was sprawled out in the middle of the bed in nothing but his briefs. Quickly, Jack pulled the bed sheet up over him, not that he was modest but because this was just damned awkward. Everything about tonight had been awkward. "How about I go to the other room, you keep your dog in here with you, and we both try to make the most of what little bit of night we've got left? Oh, and so you know, if I wanted a woman—which I don't—I wouldn't have to sneak into her bed."

"You mean like you just sneaked into *my* bed?" she asked, laughing.

Jack slid toward the edge of the bed, where Bella was already stretched out and snoozing. And wouldn't be budged when he tried. "On second thoughts, you go take the other bed. And take your dog with you." He looked her straight in the eye, grateful she hadn't asked him why he was only now crawling into bed, and what he'd been doing for the past few hours. Because, truthfully, sitting alone on the side of the road, intermittently crying then cursing himself, wasn't something he wanted to admit to. "Oh, and turn off the light on your way out."

She did. But before she left, she paused for a moment, and gave him the most sympathetic look he'd ever seen in his life. "Whatever it is, Jack, I'm sorry. If you need anything, please let me know. I don't have a lot of friends in this world, but I do know how to be a good one."

Her words drew him in and wouldn't let him go to sleep, even though his body was exhausted. They were words that made him wonder, even more, why he wanted to be around Carrie as badly as he did. But he did. That was the thought that eventually floated him off to sleep. He liked being with Carrie. As a friend. Maybe even…

And, yes, he'd had that *other* thought when they'd been kissing. The same one she'd had. The same one he was having right now, that was shoving him out of bed and down the hall to a cold shower and a long night of restlessness.

CHAPTER SIX

THE DAY ARRIVED too early, and so did the patients. By the time Jack had finally managed to doze off, a stray rooster outside had been crowing its morning welcome, very obnoxiously. "Damn," he'd muttered, refusing to open his eyes to the light creeping in through a parting in the curtain. He was used to rough nights, but the one he'd finally escaped had been rougher than any that had assaulted him in the past five years. Things he hadn't dreamed before, hadn't thought of since then had come back to him. And new things…

This morning he felt worse than if he'd drunk out half a tavern. Except he hadn't drunk. Didn't touch the damned stuff because he knew that if he did, he'd never stop. He'd get himself lost in the bottle and never find his way back out. Probably wouldn't even want to because… Too much.

Too much Evangeline here. Too much Alice. His home. His family. Too much of everything that had ever meant anything to him that had been gone in the blink of an eye while he'd slept in. Unforgivable.

He'd promised Evangeline he'd take her to the reservation. Had assured her and reassured her because she hadn't liked making that drive by herself. Yet when the time had come, he'd made another choice. To sleep. And maybe Winona was right when she'd said that the village had taken too much of him. But he'd allowed that to happen. Maybe as an excuse to stay away since he hadn't been happy in his marriage. Or maybe he'd liked being of service. He didn't remember now. Didn't remember anything except the look of hurt on Evangeline's face that morning when he'd rolled over in bed to go back to sleep after she'd just begged him to drive her.

The last look. And he'd never said goodbye. Not to Evangeline. Not to Alice. "Alice," he whispered, his voice trembling. He hadn't kissed his little girl goodbye. That was what hurt the most.

So now he deserved to live with the memories of what he'd done. He also deserved all the ghosts that haunted him, and to be reminded every day what a waste he was. What a failure.

Jack sat up on the edge of the bed and dropped his feet to the cold wooden floor. He braced himself to stand, then looked out the bedroom window, saw the sun. He hated the sun when he felt this way. Hated life. Then he stood, tugged on his jeans and shirt, stretched, grabbed his personal backpack and headed down the hall, trying to psych himself up for what he had to face this morning. More patients would be waiting. At least twenty of them who'd come yesterday but had started a list for today when they hadn't been seen.

It was always like that at Saka'am. Too much need, not enough of anything to go around. That was why Evangeline had chosen to return here to live. She'd been a social worker who'd wanted to make a difference. She'd had ideals. Dreams. Hopes for the future of her little hometown. Hopes for the future of her people. And now…

He looked at himself in the mirror, then looked away. There was nothing there he wanted to see.

"You ready for work?" he called, when he heard Carrie's footsteps in the hall.

"Yep. Someone left muffins and coffee for us, in case you're interested."

Her cheerful voice annoyed him. And when he stepped back into the hall, the optimism shining on her face annoyed him almost as much. "You go on. I'll be right behind you."

"Are you always so grumpy in the morning?" she persisted.

"Usually."

"That's too bad, because mornings are the best part of the day. You know, new outlook, new opportunities. Wake up on the right side of the bed some morning and you might find you like it."

"What I like is two cups of coffee and solitude in the morning."

"Well, I can accommodate you on both. Coffee's in the kitchen and solitude starts right now." With that, she walked straight to the front door, Bella trailing along after her, then went outside.

The door banged behind her and Jack flinched. He dragged himself to the kitchen for his coffee. Damn morning, he thought as he plodded back to the bedroom to pick up his belongings. Stupid, damn morning.

Heading into his own exam area, Jack pushed back the curtains and was greeted by Arthur Two Crows and Bella, sitting there looking silly happy. *Great*, he thought. *Can't have the girl, but I get her damned dog as a consolation prize.* "Carrie," he yelled across the room. "Would you *please* come get your dog? She's in my exam area."

"Her name's Bella," Carrie called back.

"Carrie mentioned you weren't in the best mood this morning," Palloton said, stepping outside on the stoop to stand next to Jack, who was taking a break.

"Bad memories."

"I wondered about that. In fact, I've wondered why you even came here. Figured you were just into a harder than ever punishment phase."

Jack looked out into the middle of the road where Chief Charley had taken up his post, standing there, arms folded across his chest, still scowling, still watching. "Actually, I was hoping it wouldn't be so hard. You know that saying about time healing all wounds."

"Only if you let it, Wiwa. Look, last time we talked—what was it? A month before you came back. Anyway, you told me then you needed something different, and I told you to be a heron. In Native American cultures, the heron is a symbol of good luck and patience. I like that interpretation. But in some areas the heron is a restless loner, probably because herons in nature are solitary creatures." He chuckled. "Except during breeding times. So, when I told you to be a heron, I didn't mean the one who is the restless loner. I meant the one who is a symbol of good luck and patience. Because that's who you are. And you'll see that again once you become the heron."

"Did they teach you that in law school, Palloton?" Jack asked bitterly.

Palloton laughed. "No. That's what life has taught me so far. And it's taught you the same thing. You simply can't see it right now."

"What I see is what I ought to see. Nothing more."

"Those were difficult days. But you're tough enough to get through them. If you let yourself."

"Easy to say, but everything I'm doing lately feels like I'm lost, with no direction. I knew I had to come back to face it. To face myself. But it's not working."

"It's about the climb, Jack. The struggles may knock you down right now, but you've got to keep trying because at some point you're going to make it to the top. And I promise you, the view, when you get there, will be worth the effort. That's where you'll see the true heron."

"*If* I get there."

"The question is, do you want to get there?"

"I didn't for a long time. But now..." He shrugged. Shook his head. Let out a heavy sigh.

"Well, Carrie said you were out late last night. You should have called me, Wiwa. No way I would have let you do what you were doing alone. In case you've forgotten, I've got your back. Always have, always will."

"And I appreciate that. But last night...no big

deal. Just couldn't sleep so I went for a long walk."

"You went *there*, didn't you? Where it happened?"

"I might have." Jack patted his old friend on the shoulder as he stepped around him. "And as far as your heron goes, maybe you should have called me Nko'o instead of Wiwa. It means single or solitary, and that's the heron I am now."

"Only if you want to be," Palloton said, turning to look at Charley. He acknowledged the man with the briefest of nods and then returned to his desk. "Oh, and I'll be in Marrell week after next. A civil suit between property owners. Might stay there a few days, especially if you want to go climb Stonewall or Jasper Ridge. Sound interesting?"

"Maybe," he said, his mood beginning to lighten. "If I have time."

"Sounds like fun to me," Carrie said, in passing.

"You climb?" Palloton asked her.

She shook her head. "Not yet. But Jack's going to teach me."

"Well, you're in great hands. He's the best around. Nobody I know could ever outclimb him. Including me. And I'm pretty good."

"Give me some time," she joked, "and maybe I'll give you two a run for your money."

"You're going to have to develop some pretty good skills, especially where Jack's concerned. Once you get him on the ropes, he's a natural."

A natural, Jack thought. Maybe once. But so much of him was gone now, he didn't know what was left. Yet as he looked at Carrie, who was bubbling with enthusiasm, and so happy to be doing what she was doing, he wondered if some of the moving forward she was so keen on would work for him. Because where he was now was a place he didn't want to be. Not anymore. But he'd gone on so long being this way he wasn't sure he knew how to get out of it. Or what would be out there for him if he did, somehow, manage to move forward. "Will there be a wager involved?" he asked Palloton, finally giving in to a smile.

"When was there *not* a wager involved?" his friend answered. Then, turning to Carrie, he winked. "I always let him win."

"*You* let *me* win?" Jack laughed out loud. "In your dreams, my friend. In your dreams."

The trip back to Marrell was quiet. Jack didn't talk much. Mostly, general chitchat. Or about climbing. His mood was certainly better than it had been earlier and for that Carrie was grateful, as she hadn't looked forward to the long, bumpy ride in his gloomy cloud. And so the time passed, not quickly but not in discomfort either. But when they turned onto Marrell's main road the first thing they saw was the cloud of black smoke hanging over a crowd of people that had gathered in the street and were simply standing there. The second thing they saw were the last of the embers of what had formerly been…her apartment.

It took a minute for it to sink in that she was looking at the ashes of practically everything she owned in this world. When she finally did realize it, the only word she could manage was a very quiet "No." This couldn't be happening. Another shove backward. Not again.

Jack's response was to take hold of her hand,

then hold tight. “I’m sorry,” he said. “I’ll help you get through this, Carrie. I’m not sure what it’s going to take, but you can count on me. I promise.” He squeezed her hand even tighter, then scooted closer to her, as close as the seat divider would allow, and put his arm around her shoulder. “Maybe there’s something left.”

“I didn’t have much to begin with, so I doubt it. I mean, except for Bella, my old truck and what I have in my backpack…everything in there was my entire life.” No, she didn’t have much in terms of possessions. Clothes, a couple of mementoes from her past. Her school books… Still, this was her life gone up in flames, the way it always had. And she was angry and hurt and scared because this should have been a fresh start. “So, what do I do now?” she asked, glad for the hand that still held hers because she was so close to tears she didn’t want to shed. Those tears would mean defeat, and she wouldn’t be defeated. Although she felt so close to it right now. Which made her appreciate Jack’s reassurance, even though she didn’t have anything left to be reassured about.

"For starters, move in with me. My lifestyle is pretty…sparse. But I've got a spare room and a bed, and it's yours, if that's what you want to do."

His gesture touched her. Every time she'd been kicked to the ground before, there'd been no one there to help her back up. But that was what Jack was doing. He was holding out his hand to her and she didn't know how to respond to that. "That might work for a day or two, but what about next week? Or next month? What do I do about that? I mean, how can I even take your course? My books were in there, and I can't afford to replace them."

Jack moved even closer to her to allow her to put her head on his shoulder. Which she did, without hesitation. "We'll figure it out, Carrie. I know I'm not very good at the friendship thing, but I want to help you."

"Because you want me in Saka'am?"

"Because I want you to fulfill something in yourself that I'm not able to fulfill in myself."

"I…I don't know what to say," she said, swiping back tears that finally let go. Tears she no longer wished to fight. "Except…do you have indoor plumbing?" She was so discouraged yet so grateful to have Jack step in for her the way he was, even if she didn't understand it. Maybe, though, she didn't have to. Maybe it was a simple gesture of kindness…the kindness Palloton had spoken of. The kindness the people of Saka'am knew in him. The real Jack Hanson.

He chuckled. "Electricity, too. The whole package. Including an extra toothbrush, if you need it."

"That one I've got. Along with one set of clothes, my hairbrush and an extra pair of shoes."

"Then that's your start," he said. "And whatever you don't have, or will need right away, we'll get it."

It was a nice offer, and she desperately wanted it to be sincere. But in her experience nice offers always turned into bad things. The philanthropist who'd offered to put her through nursing school but had expected *favors*, which she wouldn't grant. The police sergeant who'd offered to put in a promotion recommendation for her if she covered up an impropriety of his, which she wouldn't do. The foster mother who'd offered her a permanent home in exchange for what amounted to little more than slavery, which she'd refused to submit herself to. Yes, nice offers on the surface that came with all sorts of consequences and, right now, she didn't want another consequence to face. Especially not from Jack.

"I've never had anybody just offer me anything without wanting something in return," she said, still swatting at her tears. "And I have nothing to give in return. So, while I appreciate what you're trying to do, I'm really good at starting over. I've had lots of practice. Which means I can handle this on my own, Jack. You don't have to be bothered with me."

"I'm not bothered with you, Carrie. I know you think I am, and I'm sure I come off that way, but I'm not, and you don't have to handle this on your own. I *can* help you. And your dog."

"Her name's Bella." Carrie took one final look at the burnt pile of her life, then shut her eyes to it. It was time to move on—again. But this time in an unforeseen direction.

* * *

Jack brought his truck to a stop in front of his cabin. Like so many of the other cabins around there, it was log with a green tin roof and a substantial set of steps up to the front porch. It was two stories high, surrounded by nothing except grass and prairie shrubs. "Can you cook?" he asked, as he helped her out.

She looked around, liked what she saw. The openness, especially. She'd never lived anywhere so open before, and as far as she could see in every direction there were no cars or people or buildings. Just nature. To a city girl, so much nature all around her was wonderful. Liberating. She drew in a deep breath of fresh Montana air and savored the essence of it for a moment before she let it back out. "Not really. I can open cans, and I'm good with the microwave, but in my life..." She shrugged. "Never had the chance to learn. This is amazing, Jack. I expected...well, not this."

He laughed. "Not everything reflects my personality. I liked this place when I was a kid. Saw potential here. It was always in rough shape, but when I got the chance to buy it, I did, and fixed it up. Some things are worth the effort to bring back."

"Is that how you see me? As someone worth the effort to bring back?"

"I see you as someone who's worth a lot more than she thinks she is. Someone who doesn't see the potential in herself that I see."

"Do you really see that much potential in me?" It pleased her to know he did because that validated her and she desperately wanted to be validated by him.

"Maybe not in your domestic skills, but as a medic you have what it takes, Carrie. It may be a little rough around the edges at times, but it's all there. Instinct, skill, desire. All of it. But since you can't cook..." He cocked an amused eyebrow. "Any chance you can clean?"

She was over the moon happy he saw that in her when no one else ever had. That meant he was looking at her closely, and she liked it that he was. "Yes. I'm probably not as organized as you'd prefer, but I'm tidy, and I do like to keep everything clean. Living on the streets in filth will do that to you. Oh, and I'll do the laundry. Not that I'll have much of it myself. But it goes along with that whole cleanliness thing… Having clean clothes when I grew up was a luxury, and I don't take washing them for granted now."

"Laundry's good. And what about coffee?" he asked.

"I make great coffee." OK, that was a lie. Her coffee was horrible. She knew it. But she didn't want to let him down. Besides, if she practiced, she'd improve. That was what her life had been about—practicing to improve.

"Then that's the arrangement. Cleaning and coffee."

"And you throw in everything else? Seems like I'm getting the best of this deal."

"I'm happy with what I'm getting," he said, as he opened the front door. "If we stick to the agreement, everything will be fine."

"What you're getting is me, and I'm not easy. In fact, I lied about the coffee. I can't make it. It always ends up tasting like mud."

"Did you lie about the laundry?" he asked, fighting back a smile.

"No. That's something I *can* do."

"Then let's make that the agreement. You get the laundry and the cleaning, I get everything else."

"You're too kind," she said, finally feeling better about the situation. This was the part of Jack she really liked. The lighter, friendlier, understanding side. Not that she didn't like the darker parts but they were more difficult to deal with as he wouldn't let her close to them. This part, though, was lovely. He made her feel cared for, and cared about. Made her feel like she mattered to him in ways other than being his student, or someone he had work plans for somewhere down the road.

Most of all, it made her feel like she belonged here. And for someone who'd never belonged anywhere before, that was an overwhelming feeling. One that caused her to hope for things she'd never dared hope for. So, maybe everything would turn out better than she could have ever expected but had always wanted.

"Let me hear you say that after you've lived with me a couple of days."

"You're not that bad," she said, heading for what she believed was the kitchen. "There used to be this cat in my neighborhood. If she saw you coming near her, she'd puff all up, try to make herself larger than she was, hoping that would scare you off. It was the only defense she had against people she didn't want around her, people she was afraid of. But if you could get near, the puff went down, and she'd snuggle on your lap and purr. Palloton may think you're a heron, but I think you're that pussycat. So, let me try the coffee. I might get lucky." She giggled as Bella bounded into the cabin, went straight to Jack, then leaned against his leg. "And it looks like Bella thinks she's getting pretty lucky, too."

"Get your damned dog off me," he said. "That's the other part of this arrangement. You do the laundry and the cleaning, *and* you keep your dog away from me. If you can do that, we'll get along."

Carrie smiled as she coaxed Bella away. Amidst the shock of losing everything, and the fear of what was ahead for her, she was actually happy. And if it had been appropriate in any way, she would have thrown her arms around his neck and given him a great big kiss. *Again.* But the first time he'd called it inappropriate and had said they couldn't do it again. So she wouldn't. Although she really wanted to.

"I haven't done as much with it as I hope to in the future, but it's clean, warm and the roof doesn't leak." Jack stood back and let Carrie enter her new bedroom. It had a bed and a table lamp but no table. There was a stack of hangers in the closet, a mirror on the back of the door and a plastic bin with drawers, possibly for her undies. He'd intended this room for a study, after he got his own decorated, but he hadn't done that yet. It was pretty much the same as this one, without the storage bin and the mirror. Most of his clothes were folded in cardboard boxes and his table lamp had a crack in its porcelain base.

None of that mattered, though, as his goal was to exist, not to live. Except now he did wish he had a little more to offer Carrie.

"This is nice," she said, dropping her bag of

new clothes on the bed, along with the two scrub outfits she'd borrowed from the hospital.

"Not really. I don't need much, and I don't care what I surround myself with. So I keep it basic. But if there's anything you need…"

"I'm fine," she said. "I'm a lot like you in that I don't have a lot of needs either. You don't get to have needs when you're bounced around the way I always was. So this is good."

"Well, there's an extra set of towels in the bathroom…sorry, we're going to have to share the bathroom. But, please, stay away from the coffeepot." They would get along, he decided. They had to. Because in Carrie he captured a glimpse of something he'd never had, but had always wanted. Optimism. She simply bounced back no matter what. He didn't, and he hoped some of that might rub off on him.

"You don't have to rub it in," she said, dropping down on the bed. "I know my limitations. But I overcome them, Jack. One of these days you're going to be telling me how I make the best coffee you've ever had."

"You've got a long way to go on that one, Carrie. To be honest, I don't predict good things."

"Yeah, well, just wait. And, in the meantime, I saw the log pile outside. Which means we heat by wood?"

"Not sure yet. The house doesn't have a central heat source, and right now a wood fire works, but I may have to upgrade. Believe it or not, I like my creature comforts."

"Better watch yourself, Jack. You're giving away too much of yourself to me."

He chuckled. "Trust me. You know nothing."

"Trust me, I know more than you think."

Which scared him. But not as badly as it might have a few days ago. "Only if I confirm what you're thinking. Which I won't."

"Whatever you say, *pussycat*. So, can I go chop you some wood?"

"You know how to handle an ax?"

"I'm a tactical paramedic. I've had to knock down a few doors in my time. So, yes, an ax was required."

Jack suddenly smiled, picturing his intrepid little paramedic with an ax. It was a cute image.

Carrie all serious and determined, carrying that thing at her side, looking like a miniature lumberjack. His pulse picked up a beat or two, not in a sexual sense but, rather, in the sense that she was finding her way in more and more. And in such unique ways. "Well, I've got logs out back that need splitting, if you're serious."

She wrinkled her nose at him. "I'd love to split your logs."

That little bit of a flirt was more than he could stand. He had to get out of there. Go somewhere to regroup. To work. Yes, working would take his mind off, well, everything. So he hopped into his truck, sped away from his house, away from Carrie, taking care not to look in the rearview mirror lest the light in the guest bedroom window pulled him back. And he did want to be pulled back. Which was why he wouldn't allow it. Because no matter how his heart picked up a beat or two when she was near, no matter how much he was attracted, intrigued and caught up by her, he couldn't have what he wanted. That was his lot in life now. He accepted that, even in his weaker moments when he allowed Carrie to get in. There was no battle here. Nothing to win.

"Sleep well?" Jack asked Carrie, as he passed her in the hall the next morning. He was on his way out of the bathroom, hair still wet from his shower, towel wrapped around his middle, bare-chested, wondering if he should have dressed since he now had a roommate. In deference to that, he had donned the towel.

She was wearing an old T-shirt of his. It hung to her knees, was several sizes too large, and fell off her left shoulder. Sexy as hell. Something he didn't want to see, didn't want to tempt him, but he couldn't help himself. He was tempted. And more.

"Two hours wasn't enough," she said, giving him a bold stare. "Could have used a couple more, but you take what you can get when they call you in early." She tilted her head as she did an obvious scan of his body. "You've got abs, Jack. Great abs. Do you work out?"

Evangeline had always teased him for being a little on the soft side. Told him she liked her men a little tighter. But he'd never done anything about it then. Only after her death… "I did in Phoenix. Health club several times a week, all that kind of thing. Here, I just work harder."

"Well, hard work pays off." She smiled as she slid past him. "Now, for an attempt at coffee."

"Please, no," he groaned.

"It'll be good."

"It'll be good…*at the hospital*."

She stopped, then turned around. To get a better look. He knew that. Knew exactly what she was doing, even though he couldn't see it. But he could feel it, feel the burning scrutiny of her eyes, and suddenly it aroused him. Visibly. In his towel. He was glad his back was to her, not his front, as he didn't want her to see her effect on him. "Just pour some orange juice, OK?" he said, heading down the hall to his room, hoping the sweat didn't start beading on his forehead until he was out of her sight. "I'll meet you outside in half an hour, and we can go get your truck. And maybe some *good* coffee."

"Don't judge my coffee, Jack, until you've tried it."

Was it him, or was she being suggestive? He was so out of practice he didn't know. But he didn't hang around to find out. Instead, he ducked into his room, shut the door and leaned his back against it, willing his pulse to even out. This wasn't good. Not good at all.

"It's only a scratch," Carrie reassured the curly-headed little boy called Jamie, who would not look at her. He'd kept his arms folded tightly across his chest, staring at the floor, refusing to say a word for the fifteen minutes she'd been working with him in the ER. "All I need you to do is let me wash it, put some cream on it and then a bandage."

He shook his head, and Carrie looked over at Jamie's mother, who was so wrapped up in something on her cell phone she was totally unaware of what was happening with her son. "Mrs. Albright, I really need some help getting Jamie to cooperate," she said, fighting the urge to yank the phone from the mother's hand and smash it on the floor. Her *real* mother had been that way—never in the moment, never involved. And it made Carrie feel bad for Jamie because she knew what it was like to be ignored.

"Just a minute," Mrs. Albright said, waving Carrie off.

"I don't have a minute," Carrie said, her irritation now turning to anger. This whole procedure should have been finished ten minutes ago and she should have been on to her next patient by now. There were three in the queue, waiting for her. But here she was, stuck with a mom who didn't care and a scared little boy. "I have other patients who need my assistance, and you're taking up their time." She bit her lips to keep from saying what she wanted to say, that the woman was being an insensitive cow. Back in Chicago she'd have said it—and more. But in Marrell… she had to be different here. Had to be better. People expected that of her. *Jack* expected that of her.

The woman held up a finger this time to put Carrie off, and that was when the Chicago in her got riled. Instead of saying anything, she marched over to Mrs. Albright, removed the cell phone from her hand, clicked it off, then handed it back. "Cell phones are not allowed in the ER due to all the equipment we use," she said, forcing the politest voice she could muster.

"With all due respect, Nurse," the woman began, as her face turned red.

"I'm not a nurse. I'm a paramedic. And with all due respect to you, ma'am, your son needs your attention. I want to bandage his arm, and he's refusing to let me."

"If you can't handle putting a bandage on a ten-year-old boy, maybe you don't belong here," Mrs. Albright retorted.

Carrie bristled, and fought to keep herself from jumping way off the professional spectrum to take this woman on personally, but she didn't. Instead, she swallowed hard, drew in a deep breath, and forced a painful smile to her face. "What I need is to have you convince him to let me take care of his arm. It's a scratch. Not deep. No stitches required. And it will take me two minutes. After that, you can get out of here, and as soon as you're in the lobby, you can use your cell phone again."

That seemed to be the convincing argument, because Mrs. Albright stood, crossed over to

Jamie, took hold of his arm and held it out for Carrie. "There," the woman said. "Fix it. Now! I have a phone call to make."

And that was what Carrie did. Within those promised two minutes, she bandaged the scratch and Mrs. Albright and Jamie were out of there. She watched Jamie being pulled down the hall by his mother, and her heart went out to the boy, remembering the many times she'd been pulled like that.

"I heard she was giving you problems," Jack said, stepping up behind her.

Carrie's hands went into the air in mock surrender, and she smiled. "Promise, I didn't hurt her. Didn't yell, didn't slap the phone out of her hand. In fact, I acted quite…Marrell."

"As opposed to acting what?"

"Chicago. There's a difference. In Chicago, you get to be a little more…forward. People expect it, tolerate it. In Marrell, well, I haven't been here long enough to know, but I'll bet they expect proper manners most of the time."

"Well, for what it's worth, last time she brought Jamie in, I did break her cell phone. I didn't mean to, but as I was trying to persuade her to hold Jamie down, she wouldn't let go of the damn thing, and I accidentally bumped her and it hit the floor. Which worked out to her advantage, because the one I bought her was much better than the one she had before. So, as long as she walked out of here with the new one intact, everything's good. And she'll be the worst one you'll encounter tonight. Promise."

"I'm a cop, remember? I've encountered a lot worse than Mrs. Albright and, on occasion, brought them to their knees."

"Is that a threat?"

She laughed. "Nope. Just adding a notation to my résumé."

"Bringing someone to their knees. Yep, just the qualifications I'm looking for in my rescue team. So, about that…" He held out a bag for her. "Your books. I replaced them."

"You didn't have to. I have a little money, I could have—"

"Like I keep telling you, I'm serving my own interests here, Carrie. I want you to succeed because I want to keep you here. Hence the books. Oh, and I have an outfitter coming in tomorrow.

He'll get you set up with the equipment you'll need." He bent low to her ear. "And I've paid for that, too."

"Jack, this worries me. I don't want to get in so deep, in case I don't work out."

"Do you ever *not* work out, Carrie?"

"In everything I've ever wanted…no. I don't. Haven't even come close in a lot of it."

"Well, unless you do something stupid to screw up this opportunity, it's going to work out. You'll get what you want, I'll get what I want…"

But what she wanted was clearly changing. Into what, she wasn't sure. But the inclinations were getting stronger, and she wondered if there was any way they *could* work. She didn't know. Didn't have a lot of hope either. Because she didn't think his intentions were the same as hers. Maybe they had been at first. Not now, though, as hers were certainly on the move.

Nice dream, though, she thought as she showed her next patient into the examining room. One that, pretty much like everything else in her life, clearly wasn't going to work out.

CHAPTER SEVEN

SHE'D BEEN STRUGGLING with the coffeepot for ten minutes—unsuccessfully—and Jack couldn't help but smile as he hid near the kitchen door, watching her. Carrie Kellem was a lot of things—smart, funny, good at her job—but as far as having talent with anything domestic, she didn't have a clue. She was fixing breakfast or, at least, trying to. She was making a mess of something simple, but he didn't have the heart to stop her because, in the worst way, he wanted her to succeed, even though the prospect of that was slim. Still, the look of determination on her face was one he prized, one that told him she was going to be his best recruit.

She didn't give up. Even now, when she was defeated, and knew it, she was still fighting her way through. Something even he wasn't so good at. In fact, he was a quitter. That's all he'd been about these past five years. Quitting, hiding, avoiding. But not Carrie. She tackled life head-on and didn't let the obstacles slow her down.

That was what he liked; that was what he needed.

"You can come out from behind the door," she finally said, without even turning around to look at him. "I know you've got that smirk on your face—the one where you're doing a little gloating over the fact I can't even make coffee—so you might as well show yourself."

He chuckled. "I'm not gloating as much as curious," Jack said, laughing as he stepped away from the door and walked across to the table where the plate of burnt toast lay. He picked up the toast, examined both sides of it, more to tease her than anything else, then took it over to the window, opened it and then turned to face her. "You don't need to do this, you know."

"See, that's the thing. I have to do it and, one way or another, I'll figure it out."

"Suit yourself. But don't do this because of me. You've got nothing to prove, since I'm already convinced."

"What I do, Jack, I do for me. I wouldn't mind giving you a decent breakfast, but for me it's about learning how to do it, then doing it." She shrugged. "It's not an altruistic thing."

"Well, altruism aside, you still don't have to do this. I usually grab something down at Millie's." He turned back to the window and tossed the toast outside, to the birds. "In my world, eating's not a priority. It's one of those things you have to do to get by. So don't sweat it, Carrie. I really don't expect anything."

"But I do, Jack. That's the point. I always do."

He turned back to face her. "Do you ever let up on yourself?"

"What do you mean by that?" she asked, almost defensively.

"You know, give yourself a break? Take time off trying to prove yourself so you can enjoy what you've already proved?"

"That's not fair. I work hard to get what I want. That's what I'm about. Who I am. And when I find deficiencies, I try to overcome them."

"But to what end, Carrie? Will you ever be satisfied with yourself?"

She shrugged. "I don't know. Maybe…someday. When I've found what I really want in life. But so far I haven't. So I keep looking. And looking comes with proving. But at least I'm honest with myself about who I am and what I'm doing."

"Which implies I'm not?" he asked, knowing he should take offense but not able to because she was spot-on. He didn't have it in him to be honest about himself. Not any more. He wasn't sure he even wanted to get it back, even if he could.

"Which implies nothing. We all make our choices. And while you think mine are too difficult, I think yours are." She smiled. "So, on that note, either I can take another stab at breakfast or we can meet at Millie's."

How could she be so optimistic, given what she'd been through? He didn't understand that kind of optimism or courage. But to look at her standing there, so bright, so eager to get it right, he had to admit he'd just lost a little piece of his heart to her. He only wished his heart wasn't so hardened, because Carrie deserved more than that. "Millie's sounds good. But I need to make a couple of house calls first. I've got some driving to do, so it'll probably be closer to lunch." He glanced at his watch. "I'll text you when I'm on my way there."

"Good. That gives me time to get at your woodpile."

Jack walked away smiling, shaking his head in amazement. She didn't quit. No matter what, she simply didn't give up. He'd forgotten what that felt like, but seeing it in Carrie made him realize, even more, that this should be his time, too. Carrie had certainly turned it into her time, but he wasn't sure he knew how to turn it into his. And parts of him wanted to. But would the parts that didn't want that overpower the parts that did? Because, for the past five years, the parts that wanted to hold him back had won. Too easily.

"Did you get that wood chopped?" Jack asked, dropping into the booth seat across from Carrie.

She was sure he hadn't expected her to, but she had. Quite quickly, after thirty minutes of good, hard exercise. It had felt good doing something useful and rigorous. Even the ER didn't give her the physical challenge she liked…but good, old-fashioned hard work had hit the spot and made her muscles work again. Also, it had lifted her spirits because being part of something that wasn't merely tied up in her own little world was good. It energized her. "Enough for a week," she said, picking up the menu and opening it to the lunch section. "I stacked it on the porch, so we won't have to carry it so far when we need it. I fixed the door threshold, too. It was coming up and I didn't want anybody to trip on it. Oh, and I started a load of laundry."

"Seriously, all that? In, what, four hours?"

"I like to work." It was all she'd ever known and she'd discovered, when she wasn't much older than seven or eight, that the harder you worked, the more you advanced. And she'd always wanted to advance. So she'd always worked.

"Well, I'm sorry I'm later than I'd expected, but a couple of my patients hailed me on the street…" He shrugged. "What can you do? It's Marrell, that's the way they are here. Anyway, I'm free for the rest of the day, so I was wondering if you'd like to do some climbing."

"Really?" She wasn't sure she was ready for it, but she sure didn't want to pass up the opportunity. "Before classes start?" That was still a few days off, after Caleb and Leanne Carsten returned to Sinclair.

"I'll keep it basic. Easy rock face, easy climb. Up at a place called Eagle Pointe. I used to go there when I was a kid. In fact, it's where Priscilla would take me when she was teaching me. The view is spectacular, and it's a nice hike up. So, I thought if you're up to it…"

"Oh, I'm up to it. But are you up to me?"

He chuckled. "I suppose I'm about to find out."

"But I haven't had my appointment with the outfitter. I don't have what I need…"

"It's taken care of. He'll see you after lunch, get you fixed up, and with any luck we'll be headed out in a couple of hours."

"Except I can't pay for the equipment yet. I know you said you'd take care of it, but I don't want that. I don't like charity, and that's what it is, even when you tell me there's a motive behind it." And that was a huge obstacle, as she didn't want to be indebted to anyone, including Jack, any more than she already was. In a life where no one had ever done her any favors, he'd already exhausted his fair supply, and she didn't expect anything else. Didn't want anything else. "I was hoping with my next paycheck…"

"Consider it a loan. Come next paycheck, you can pay me back. So, any other concerns or protests?"

"Not protesting. Just being practical. So, you're covered at the hospital? I thought since both Carstens were gone, there wasn't an excess of doctors to go around."

He shook his head. "There aren't. But my mom and Henry are back in town for a few days and they're going to cover. They like retirement, but I think they miss the work. Anyway, they'll take the rest of the weekend, so I've got the time. And it's been a while since I've had any time to get on the ropes myself, so it'll be good for me since basic climbing skills will be integrated into my classes. Shall we go?"

"Are you sure you want to be saddled with a beginner? Because I'm sure you'd have a much better time without me." She was flattered. Even more than that, she was excited. Not only to start climbing but to be doing it with Jack. Alone. Not with the rest of the class. But she truly didn't want to hold him back.

"I wouldn't have asked if I didn't want to." He signaled the waitress over to the table. "I'll have an iced tea and a chef's salad."

"But we've got pot roast and mashed potatoes on special, Jack," the waitress, a woman named Janice, who frequented the hospital for migraines and other aches and pains, protested. "Don't you like our pot roast, Jack?" She licked her lips seductively.

Jack tugged uncomfortably at the collar of his denim shirt. "I love the pot roast, Janice, but I'm going to be climbing later, so I've got to keep it light."

"And I'll have the same," Carrie said, trying to hold back a giggle. Janice was being so obvious. "Climbing, too."

With a shrug, and a quick scribble on her order pad, she scooted off toward the kitchen, seemingly taking it personally that she hadn't sold the lunch special. Or scored with Jack.

"Lady in love," Carrie commented casually. She glanced over at the lunch counter, saw Janice standing behind it, glaring daggers at her. "*Really* in love."

"Yeah, well, she can keep it to herself. I'm not interested."

"In her? Or in being in love in general?"

"Both," he said. "Janice is from Westslope, where I'm from. We grew up together and, trust me, there's never been anything between us."

"Well, not for want of trying on her part. Look at her. She can't take her eyes off you, except for the occasional scowl she turns on me." Carrie picked up the glass of water on the table and took a sip. Then said, "And if looks could kill, I'd be a dead woman."

Jack shook his head. "She knows I don't date. I've told her so at least a dozen times since I've been back."

"But don't they say something about hope springing eternal?" Jack seemed embarrassed, and it was funny watching him squirm the way he was. Staunch and rigid Jack Hanson was blushing because the lady adored him. And literally tugging at his collar. He was cute, in a way she'd never seen cuteness in him before. He was vulnerable. Human. Even though he tried to hide it.

"Her hope can spring however she wants, as long as it's not springing all over me."

"Will you ever let someone back into your life, Jack? I don't know what happened with your family, and I'm not going to ask, but it seems like you've sentenced yourself to an awfully high price to pay." She really hadn't meant to turn this into something so serious, but she was curious, as Jack seemed to come in so many pieces, and it would be up to her to fit them together if she ever wanted to truly get to know him. Because he wouldn't do that himself and she really did want to get to know the whole man since, it seemed, she might have a future here. Alongside him.

"My life is fine like it is." He turned his head and looked out the window, an obvious sign that the conversation was over.

Carrie wasn't satisfied, though. For whatever reason, they were together. Maybe not in a traditional sense but together, nonetheless. This, if nothing else, made her want to know more. Made her want to know him better. She liked Jack, even if he didn't want that. In fact, she more than liked him. She cared—cared about a man who was wounded and in pain. Which hurt her heart, because she understood pain in the deepest sense. She was trying hard to fix it in herself now, but she also wanted to fix it in Jack. Or, help him fix it in himself. Because she cared. Maybe even loved him a little. "Don't look now," she whispered across the table, "but lover girl is undoing the top button on her blouse. I think she has intentions, Jack."

Jack twisted around in the booth and flagged Janice, who practically jumped over the lunch counter to get to him.

"Yes?" she asked breathlessly.

"Could you make those salads to go, please?"

Carrie bit back a smile as Janice squared her shoulders, obviously angry that they weren't staying, and marched straight back to the kitchen. "The course of love thwarted by a couple of take-out containers," she said. "Was that your intent?"

"It's always my intent when I see it headed in my direction," he snapped. *"Always."*

Surprisingly, that pronouncement stung. It wasn't that she was looking for what Janice was. She wasn't. But Jack had been so adamant about not wanting it that she felt the same rejection Janice must have been feeling. And it occurred to Carrie, for the first time, that maybe she was more than a little in love with Jack herself. Maybe she was falling into the kind of love she'd never expected to find. Or be able to give.

"It doesn't look too bad," she said, staring up at the rock he'd chosen for their first time. It had a lot of handholds and a lot of places for her toes to go, as well. Still, it looked daunting. "Shouldn't we have started with one of those indoor climbing places? You know, where they strap you in and pretty much suspend you while you climb, and if you fall they lower you down?"

"In a practical world, yes, but there's nothing like that around here, which is why we're going to start with what's called *bouldering*."

"Bouldering?" she asked.

"That's where you go up a boulder rather than a full-sized rock. It takes the least amount of time and gear, and you never get so high up that you can't just jump off comfortably. Also, climbers can traverse the rock horizontally, which will help them work on strength and movement without being intimidated by the prospect of falling too far. I've always taught it first because it requires only climbing shoes, a chalk bag, a crash pad to cushion your jump or fall off the rock, and an experienced spotter, like myself. You don't need a rope or a harness." He smiled as he approached the boulder he'd chosen. "Just stand here and memorize it for a minute, because after that you're going up, and knowing where you're going is always good. Oh, and even though your fall won't be drastic…" He patted his head. "Helmet. Get used to it."

"And the chalk is for?"

"Absorbing moisture on your hands. Slippery hands mean slipping off the rock. Also…" He pulled a roll of tape from his pocket. "In the beginning, I want you taping up. It will help protect your skin, and also add some support to your entire hand. A lot of experienced climbers don't like it because they prefer the physical contact with the rock. But to start…" He ripped off a strip of tape and applied it to her left hand. "Tape it, and play it safe. Oh, and not just any tape. This is made specifically for climbers. It has some flexibility but doesn't stretch like regular athletic tape."

She was so caught up in listening to him she hardly noticed when her hands and wrists were fully taped. Hardly noticed the shivers that went up her spine when he touched her. Hardly noticed that he was standing so close and intimately as he wrapped her hands that she could feel his body heat. But…*hardly* wasn't *not* noticing, because she did. In ways that made it hard to concentrate on what he was saying. "I assume we warm up after this?"

He nodded. "I don't do the daily kind of exercises you do but, yes, you've got to be in shape. And if you're not warmed up, you're more prone to freezing up before you get to the top. Which isn't a good thing, because we don't have a rescue team who can come and get you down. *Yet.*"

"Always trying, aren't you, Jack?" she said, looking up again at where she was hoping to be shortly. Up top, standing on the ledge, looking down. It wasn't going to be a steep or very tall climb, but conquering small goals led to conquering larger ones. And, in her life, it was always about conquering the larger ones. "So, how do I start?" she asked, bracing herself for whatever came next.

After ten minutes of warm-up exercises, Jack took her hand and pulled her over to the rock she was going to attempt. "Watch me, then do what I do. Unless I fall, then don't do that," he said, strapping on his own helmet. "Now, think about grabbing a pull-up bar. You clasp your hands around the bar and pull your feet off the ground. In climbing, that's called a *dead hang.* In other words, you suspend yourself there, in midair. It requires brute strength, especially when to climb, you've got to hang with your arms bent at an angle and your legs pretty much straight."

She looked at his arms, admiring the strength in his biceps, triceps and shoulder muscles. All the muscles she knew she'd have to use to hold her arms bent, as he was doing now. "It looks like you're using your arm muscles much more than you would if you were hanging there with straight arms." She addressed him as he was raising his legs above his head to anchor to the rock.

"Hanging with straight arms uses skeletal strength," he said, not in the least winded. "Hanging with your arms bent relies on upper-body strength, and since most beginners don't have sufficient upper-body strength to do that for very long, you do that only when you're progressing. Otherwise, instead of trying to build your biceps right off, hang down with your arms straight and legs bent when you're between moves. You'll save your energy for when you want to keep going. Now…" He turned his attention solely to the rock, did a traverse climb, alternately dead hanging and progressing. Then, instead of trying for the top, which was only about fifteen feet up, he dropped himself off the rock and landed feetfirst. Brushing off his hands, he unstrapped his helmet and smiled at her. "Not as glorious as climbing to the top, but we'll save that for next time. Today I want you going from side to side."

And here she'd had visions of heading straight to the top, then standing there, surveying her domain below. Hands on hips, head thrown back in bold conquest. The mighty rock climber in her triumph. But his vision was something akin to a spider crawl, six feet above the ground, trying to figure out what was supposed to be bent or at an angle. Which proved to be more of a challenge than she'd expected, as her first seven or eight times up on the rock she fell off straightaway. Thank heavens for the crash pad, or else she'd already have a very sore back and hips. Not to mention rear end, which unceremoniously took the brunt of most of her falls.

"But you made it look so easy," she said, standing up from yet another fall.

"Because I've been doing it since I was a kid."

"Did you fall off this much at first?" she asked, as she wobbled to her feet. This time he helped her, taking hold of her arm to give her an assist to her feet. And didn't let go of her arm after she was steady. Rather, he held on, stared into her eyes, and for an instant she expected…well, she wasn't exactly sure what she expected. Or hoped for. A kiss maybe?

But that wasn't to be. "Let me give you a boost," he finally said, after a long pause. Then dropped her arm.

"You couldn't have given me a boost several falls ago?" she asked, trying to force her concentration back. It wasn't easy, however. Not with Jack standing so close to her. Not with the lingering tingle of his hand on her arm.

"I could have. But you need falling experience, as well as climbing. Now's as good a time as any to get it."

She rubbed her aching backside. "I so appreciate your consideration."

He laughed. "You'll thank me for it later."

"I don't ever thank anybody who lets me fall." She reached up and took hold of the same spot she'd grabbed every time before. "So, boost me."

He got himself under her and pushed her up, holding her steady with his back. "Now move."

"To where?" she asked, liking the feel of his support.

"Look up, spot your next move, then go there."

She looked forward, spotted her next logical handhold and grabbed on, then forced her feet to follow—with his assistance, of course. She tried it again and again until, quicker than she'd expected, she crossed the rock. She was totally on the other side of it, which felt as good as if she'd scaled it to the top. "Can I come down now?" she asked, simultaneously letting go, falling on top of him, then rolling on the ground, wrapped in his arms. "You're not as soft as the crash pad," she said, making no attempt to extricate herself.

And he made no attempt to unwind himself from her. In fact, his arms wrapped around her a little tighter. And his knee moved up to trap hers under his.

"Is this part of the lesson?" she asked, as she lifted her head to take his kiss. The kiss that parted her lips and explored the recesses of her mouth like they'd never been explored before. She was glad for the biceps and triceps that were wrapped around her. Not to mention his quadriceps femoris, iliopsoas, Sartorius and all those other leg muscles that were covering hers.

First lesson, perfect ending, she thought. Perfect first kiss, perfect first...*this.* Maybe it wasn't meant to be a permanent thing. She didn't know. But right now she was all about living in the moment. Maybe for the first time in her life there was nothing to think through. Or nothing to plan ahead.

In answer, he reached over to remove her T-shirt, but she laid a hand on his to stop him. "Not here," she said.

He raised a speculative eyebrow but didn't question her. And maybe someday she'd tell him why. That the fantasy she'd had of this moment—and, yes, she'd had the fantasy—didn't happen at the foot of a rock. It was...romantic. Maybe wine and candlelight. Soft music. She'd never had a fantasy of being with a man before. In fact, she hadn't allowed herself fantasies at all, ever—until Jack. Because in her life they couldn't have come true.

And if this was her only time with him, which it might be, she wanted it to be perfect. She wanted a perfect memory of a perfect moment. With Jack, she knew it would be perfect. Was that the fantasy of a woman in love? She didn't know. But that didn't matter as it was a fantasy she wanted to make real, even if only for a little while.

The warm water on her body felt good. Being naked in that warm water, with Jack, felt… strange. A good kind of strange, though. The urgency of the moment they'd had out on the rocks was gone, replaced by a different sensation. More relaxing. For her, even more arousing. Good wine. Dim lights. Soft music. No, she wasn't getting those. That part of the fantasy wasn't happening, but the real part was. The shoulder massage. The long, lingering kisses. The tenderness and patience being shown by someone who was very experienced to someone who was not so much. Someone who took away everything in her past and helped her to experience the pure pleasure of the moment.

She'd thought about this. Maybe not so much in real terms as in fantasy ones, but there was something in his brooding she understood, something she wanted to touch… And she'd wanted him to want her the way she wanted him. But there'd been no indication, nothing to show her that he was interested in any kind of way, let alone that. And now this. It was where she wanted to be. Under him, on top of him…maybe a little in his heart. "Are you sure?" she asked him, as he pulled her up to her feet, and they stood pressed together, naked, wet.

"No." He wrapped a towel around her, his hands slow and steady as he pulled it across her breasts, taking care to skim his fingertips lightly over them before he secured the towel. Then he stepped out of the tub, and stood there for a moment simply staring at her. Jack, in his naked beauty, looking so intense, so full of thoughts. "Are you?" he finally asked, extending a hand to help her out.

"Yes," she said, moving closer to him. "I'm not…well, let's just say I'm not a woman of the world. But, yes, I'm sure I want this."

He pulled her roughly to his chest. "And you always get what you want."

"I try," she murmured against his lips. "I surely do try."

CHAPTER EIGHT

SHE WAS BEAUTIFUL, sitting on the side of his bed, putting on her shirt. No apparent afterthoughts or guilt over what they'd done. In fact, she'd been rather bold about it. No shyness, no inhibitions. It had been nothing like he'd ever experienced. The freedom. The pure joy of touching and feeling and exploring. In his married life these moments had been…planned. Carrie had been so giving, which had made him want to give everything.

From the moment she'd fallen into his arms up on that boulder, he'd thought to hell with plans and guilt and all the other things that weighed him down. She'd pulled him into what she wanted, made him want the same thing, too. Made him put aside, for a little while, everything that held him back.

And now, watching her, he loved it that Carrie Kellem was her own woman. It was refreshing. Natural. Were the circumstances different, he would have welcomed it back. But he didn't. Spontaneous moments like this were good, but buried beneath them was…him. And now he was full of the afterthoughts, and guilt. Not because of any vows he'd made to himself after Evangeline had died but because he'd never made himself available to her the way he had to Carrie. Their marriage had been cordial, not passionate. He'd gotten her pregnant and had done the honorable thing, hoping the rest would come. But it never had.

And now, with Carrie, there was so much passion. She was so open, and in a lot of ways naive. And with that he feared there would be an aftermath. Or expectations. Or worse…hopes and dreams.

Wasn't that the way it always worked? It had with Evangeline. They'd dated casually. Friendship, some sex. Then…Alice, which had made their circumstances entirely different. But with Carrie… Damn, he didn't know. He just didn't know. "You OK?" he finally asked as he pulled on his cargos.

"A little surprised," she said, "but good." She smiled at him. "And you?"

No way he could tell her the truth, that he'd enjoyed every moment with her. It had been amazing. She'd been amazing. But now his world was crashing down around him. What the hell had he been thinking? What the hell had he done? "Good," he said, wishing he could bask in the afterglow or stretch out and simply hold her. Kiss her. Tell her things he'd never said before. Romantic notions. But his reality was that he lived with her now, and he was going to make sure nothing like this happened again. Besides the personal feelings that went along with it, there were also the professional ethics.

Who was he kidding? The instant she'd fallen into his arms, the only thing he'd wanted was her. And not just the physical aspects. While they were nice, it was also nice to simply connect again. But he couldn't let that last. He wasn't in the emotional place for it and didn't want to drag her into it with him. "Like I said before, you know we can't do this again, don't you?"

She stood, and stepped into her cargos, adjusted her T-shirt, then gave him a long, pointed stare before she spoke. "I figured that would be the case. It always is, isn't it?"

"What do you mean by that?" He stood as well, but took great pains not to get too close to her. Because to do that would be to succumb. He wanted to. Dear God, he wanted to. But he couldn't, because somewhere in the mix of the afternoon he'd come to terms with the fact that he had feelings for Carrie. And while he wasn't ready to admit it was love, he would admit that what was happening to him now had never happened before. But with those feelings came his need to protect her…from him. Which meant pulling back or pushing away.

She shrugged. "Nobody stays, Jack. They get what they want and they move on to something else."

She was so pragmatic it almost choked him. How often had she been hurt in her life? He'd certainly never meant to add to the toll, but that was what she thought this was. Just another time in a long, long line. "Not everybody," he said, as a lump of cold, hard sadness pounded his chest. "You just haven't found the right one."

"Or I have, and he wants no part of it…or me."

"I don't have anything to give you, Carrie. Not emotionally. Not since…" All these years, and he'd never spoken their names. He couldn't. He wasn't worthy enough to. "It's complicated."

"Not really. You've stopped moving ahead. Contented yourself with the punishment you think you deserve, the punishment you heap upon yourself every day. But you loved them, Jack. Your wife and daughter. Which means you're capable of loving someone else. Only if you want to, though."

"And if I don't?"

"Then you're right where you're always going to be. Stuck. And what we did here—since it seems to be of no consequence to you, I'm quite capable of making it just as inconsequential. What I don't want, though, is for this to affect my training. I like it here and I'm not about to let this afternoon take that away from me. I wanted to make love to you because I am falling in love with you. What you do with that is up to you.

What I'll do with that—well, I don't know yet. But my feelings for you, and maybe even your feelings for me, are standing as a pretty sturdy barrier between us, rather than breaking down the barriers the way love should. So, to make things easier on both of us, I'll find someplace else to live and sit in the back row of your class so you won't have to notice me so much.

"But one last thing, Jack. You have feelings for me. You're not hiding them too well. And you're also not hiding the fact that you don't want to have them." She moved around him, then headed out into the hall but stopped before she'd gone too far. "I've got feelings, too. Most of the people I've had in my life haven't known that, but I do. And I'm as good at hiding them as you are. You don't have to worry, though. As far as this afternoon goes, I'm over it. I'm moving on because that's what I always do. I *always* move on. I hope you can, too."

Then she left. She walked down the hall, packed her few belongings and walked out of his house with her dog. "Why not?" he said, watching from his bedroom window as she headed to town. Now he was alone again. Now he had plenty of time to think about all the ways he deserved this. Deserved worse, for turning a nice afternoon into misery, the way he had done. The heck of it was, he might have been falling in love with her, too. At least, it seemed like he was. One perfect afternoon—maybe the only perfect afternoon he'd ever had—then he'd gone and spoiled it. Another reason to feel not good enough. As Evangeline had said to him, the last time he'd ever heard her voice, *"Jack, why can't you just do better for once?"*

Good question. Why couldn't he?

A week in class now, and Carrie was nothing more than a student, the one in the back row who hoped to go unnoticed, as she'd promised him. And it was working, as other than getting her to answer a few requisite questions, Jack had totally ignored her. Which was what she wanted. But she felt a little empty because of it. And totally alone.

She was living above Millie's Diner now, hating it because Bella wasn't allowed inside, and *she* wasn't allowed to make noise after nine o'clock. Not that she was a noisy person, because she wasn't. But it made Carrie feel like she had to walk on tiptoe in her own apartment, and she even got paranoid about running the shower after cutoff time.

Plus, it was like she was doing the walk of shame every time she had to pass Janice. The way that woman scowled at her… Sometimes, Carrie swore she'd hear her growl. But she did understand love unrequited now, so she sympathized with Janice, who was feeling the same thing because of the same man.

"It's temporary," she told Bella, as they sat together on the back stoop. "Another seven weeks and we'll be doing something different. I promise, girl." Leaving Marrell for Saka'am, she hoped.

The night was wearing on and Carrie hated to go to bed, but it was going on to nine o'clock, which meant that the Millie-imposed silence was about to commence, and it was hard being silent when the floors creaked as she walked around on them, or the pipes groaned when she turned on the tap for a glass water. So she scratched Bella's, head then stood, torn between going back inside and taking another walk, even though she and Bella had just come back from one. "I wish I had a better solution than this," she told her dog. "But there aren't many options around here."

"You could move back in," Jack said, stepping out of the shadows.

"What are you doing here?" she said, not sounding any too friendly even though her heart skipped a beat.

"I came to apologize."

"Nothing to apologize for. You have a perfect right to feel the way you feel. It's got nothing to do with me, even though I made the mistake of seeing something where there's nothing. I assumed something I shouldn't have assumed."

Bella sidled up to Jack and leaned against his leg. He didn't shove her away. Instead, he reached down and scratched her behind her ears. "I'm a mess, Carrie. I have been for a long, long time. And I hurt the two people I loved most in the world. Hurt them deeply." When they'd been alive to be hurt.

"Your wife and daughter?"

He didn't acknowledge the question, neither did he deny it. "I've made some choices that weren't the easiest, but it's how I get along. How I have to get along, and I don't want this to get serious between us because, us, together, can't be one of those choices. You've got so much potential, so much life ahead of you, and I'm not able to be part of that, other than what I'm doing now. You've got a lot of higher ground ahead of you and I'm most of the way down the other side of it. I can't drag you down with me."

"Be sure before you close that door, Jack. Because once you do, I won't open it again. That's not me. I move on, I look for something else. It's probably my self-defense mechanism to keep me from getting hurt again, but I can't move back in with you because, if I do, that's not putting things into proper perspective. It'll become too easy. We'll forge some kind of laid-back relationship where I'll make bad coffee and we'll have great sex. It's not what I want for myself.

"I want…stability. I've never had it, I've never had any kind of permanence. Most of the time that's fine. Most of the time I don't even want it. But there are times when I do. Times when I want to belong somewhere. Maybe even with someone. But not with you, Jack, because you don't want the same things I do. You want to avoid, while I'm trying to embrace. And I can't be in this…this…whatever it is we've got going on between us, knowing that I must still face the world out there on my own. I've done that, and I'm not going to keep doing it forever. So, no, I'm not coming back."

"But after the training, are you staying? Or did I ruin that, too?"

"There was nothing to ruin, Jack, because nothing got started. And as for staying, yes, if I can go to Saka'am, as you said I might. But the one thing I won't do, Jack, is let time stand still for me the way you let it do for you. My goal is always to get past the pain, while your goal is to stand around and let it beat you down. I can't be part of that. I can't watch it. I can't watch what it does to you because, yes, I do care for you. More than I should. More than you would want me to." She hadn't wanted to say these things, but she had to, as with one little push she'd give in to all the things she didn't want, just because Jack was the one doing the pushing.

He nodded. "I wish it could be different," he said.

"So do I," she whispered, hoping he wouldn't see the tears forming in her eyes since it was dark out now, and tears were best saved for the dark.

"How about I keep your dog for you while you're staying at Millie's? That way, she wouldn't have to be tied outside. She could have my spare bed. And you could come see her anytime you want."

The tears did start to fall then and she brushed them back. "Her name's Bella. And, yes, I'd like that, if you don't mind."

He reached over and brushed a tear off her cheek. "I don't mind," he said tenderly. "Look, Carrie, all I can do is be honest. My life, my past…it's too complicated to have someone else involved with it. I've reconciled myself to what I can have, and I never should have stepped over that line with you. Or even come close to it. I'm sorry."

"I know," she said, handing Bella's lead over to him. "Bella's been fed for the evening, so I'll stop by in the morning, before class, with her bag of food and maybe take her for a walk, if that's OK with you."

"Anytime," he said, bending down to attach the lead to Bella's collar. "And she'll be fine."

"I know," Carrie said sadly, wishing that she, too, would be fine. But she wouldn't. She loved Jack. And he loved her back. Nothing would come of it, though. So how, in that, could she find anything fine?

Jack had already left for class by the time she arrived at his cabin to feed Bella. She'd been late, by design. She hadn't wanted to face him, not on a personal basis. Not yet. "So, I see you've moved into the spare room," she said to her dog, who was stretched out on the bed like it was hers.

Bella thumped a lazy tail but made no move to get up. "Have you already had your morning walk?" she asked, examining the dog's lead, as if that might give her the answer. "And breakfast? Did Jack get up and fix you breakfast?" She asked that, because her always hungry dog was not interested in the bowl of food Carrie had poured. Had he actually cooked for her?

Bella's response was to snort out a doggy sigh, stretch out even more, then close her eyes. "He's spoiling you," she said, surprised and pleased at the same time. It showed a side of Jack she hadn't expected. "And since that's the case, I'm going on to the hospital now to grab myself a cup of coffee and…" Take her usual spot in the back row? She wasn't sure about that. "I'll be back at lunch to take you out," she said, giving Bella a pat on the head, then scurrying out the door.

Fifteen minutes later, she was sitting in the first row of the tiny classroom, causing the other six students to shift their normal positions since the spots everyone chose on their first day seemed to be the spots they took every day after that.

"Classroom this morning, field this afternoon, after lunch," Jack announced on his way in the door. "We're going to go bouldering, so if you don't have your equipment with you now, I'd suggest you go get it during your lunch, because we've got a busy day ahead." He glanced at Carrie, but didn't acknowledge her any differently than he did anybody else. He did, however, compose and send her a text, right after he sat down at the desk at the front of the room.

She watched him text, then felt the vibration in her pocket so, instead of ignoring it, as she normally would in class, she pulled out her phone and read the short message: I assume you've been practicing without me?

Carrie looked up, gave him a discreet nod. Then in another few seconds felt the vibration again. And read: Are you good enough to instruct bouldering?

Again, she nodded discreetly. Because she was. She and Bella had gone up to that very same rock on Eagle Pointe every day, and she'd climbed up on that boulder and fallen off, then gotten back up again until she could not only dead hang without her muscles giving out but she could traverse the entire boulder at the same speed she'd seen Jack do it. Hours of practice, and she had it down. Now she was anxious to get to the next level. She wanted to go up that boulder instead of across it. But she wanted Jack there, not only to teach her but to see her do it. Because, yes, she wanted to impress him.

"This morning we're going to talk about rescue techniques in low-resource areas. You're all qualified medics in one specialty or another, so you have your first-aid skills down. But you won't always have access to all the fancy gear you've trained with. So I want you to start thinking about how wilderness and rescue medicine differs from urban rescue, which you're all highly qualified to do. We're going to talk about things like what to do when a quick trip to the hospital isn't an option, when you get yourself involved in prolonged patient care, severe environments and maybe even improvised equipment.

"Keep in mind that this is only an introductory course. If I hire you to stay and work here, there will be continuing education courses on a regular basis, covering everything from rafting to avalanche rescue, with a goal toward getting you certified in the field. It's a big field, and a difficult one, but it's my intention that once you finish the entire course, including the continuing education classes, you'll be among the best anywhere."

"How long do you anticipate the whole thing to take?" Carrie asked him.

"Because I want to get you all into the field as soon as possible, I'm breaking this up rather than teaching it straight through. So, conservatively, it'll take about a year. Maybe more."

"Then, if I opt to stay, I have to make that commitment?"

"If you want to get certified. As it is, certification isn't required, and I can hire anybody I want to go out and work, using the hospital as a base. But getting certified gives you the opportunity to travel, to go pretty much anywhere in the world you want to go. It's a wide-open field, and you can go as far as you wish, if you're willing to put in the time to get you there."

Was that what he wanted? For her to go someplace else? "How long have you been certified, Jack?"

"Since long before I was a doctor. And I've

been a member of an international rescue organization for years, as well as a certified instructor."

"And your specialty is…?" She knew, of course, but Jack was so reluctant to talk about himself, she doubted the rest of the class knew. More than that, she simply wanted to draw him out, get him talking about himself. He needed it, and she longed to hear something new from him. Something about his accomplishments. Something to remind him that he had worth.

"Mountain," he said, raising his eyebrows at her. "With a secondary in white water. I've spent a fair amount of time on the river, so I'm pretty good at that, too."

"Worst rescue you ever did?" she asked bluntly.

"Nothing anybody would be interested in," he said, the look on his face clearly indicating he was catching on to what she was trying to do.

"But if you're going to be teaching us what we need to do, shouldn't we have some idea of what you've had to do? I mean, knowing you're certified is one thing…it's a certificate indicating you've done something to earn it. But what, Jack? What have you done?"

A consensus muttering of yeses and head nods came from the students, and as Jack arose from his chair to come around to the front of the desk, he scowled at Carrie. But it wasn't an angry scowl, and she smiled back at him.

"Fine. One story. My worst rescue. And I'm assuming by worst you mean my most difficult, because my worst was a two-day hunt in the woods for a child…hard rain, mud every step of the way. It was cold, I got athlete's foot because my feet were never dry. Ended up with a mild case of pneumonia because my lungs never got dry either. And the kid was home, hiding out in his cellar all the time, trying to teach his parents a lesson. *That* was my worst.

"But my most difficult was getting a photographer off a mountain after he'd been mauled by a bear. He'd been bear-baiting, trying to get close-up photos. But what he got close-up was a bear who wanted the food he was baiting with. The guy's arm was half off when we got to him, he had serious internal damage, and he'd lain out in the open for a couple of days before someone came across him. He was barely alive.

"I got called to take a team in… Palloton was with me." He looked at the class to explain. "He's an old friend from childhood. We've always climbed together. Anyway, we got up there, saw the situation and realized it was going to take more than what we had to get him down. Naturally, it was snowing, which didn't help matters. The guy was in deep shock, badly infected, and by the time we got to him he didn't have enough time left in him to take him down the trail, which would have probably taken the better part of two days since we'd have to go slowly. So we decided to take him down the side of the mountain, to lower him to the ground and let a team down there get him to a helicopter. I figured that would take us about a day less than the other way."

Carrie looked around, and the rest of the students were practically on the edges of their seats, hanging on Jack's every word. She was, too, to be honest. "So, you had a litter up there?" she asked. "And everything you needed to do the climb down?"

"One of the things you'll learn is how to pack a litter for most of the situations you'll encounter, then to take that litter out with you. I had four people on my team going up. Anyway, it took us a while to get it rigged so we could lower him, but we did. I did everything I could medically, because I was the only trained medic in the group. There wasn't much I could do, though, under the circumstances. An IV for a couple of hours, some cleaning, some bandaging. Stitches. Anyway, we got him ready and had him lowered about forty or fifty feet, then he started thrashing. Midair, suspended several hundred feet above the ground and he was thrashing so hard his litter was beating against the rocks. Needless to say, I rigged up to climb down, but by the time I got there he was hung up on a shelf, and the litter was damaged. The pulleys wouldn't work. I couldn't get him back up, couldn't lower him down. Which meant, midair transfer. Except that meant another litter.

"Long story short, I spent the entire night on

that shelf, hanging on to the litter, tending to the guy… I'd sedated him so he wouldn't come around and cause more problems. And let me tell you, it was a miserable night. The wind got bad. The snow got worse. I was afraid he'd die of hypothermia. Afraid I'd die of it, too. Then when morning came, the area was socked in with a couple of feet of new snow. Meaning even if we did get him down, there'd be no getting a helicopter in."

"But you got the new litter?"

He nodded. "And climbing gear. Palloton came down and helped me make the transfer, but I got bumped over the edge, and couldn't get a foothold to get back up on. So I spent two hours dangling there, while the litter went down. Eventually, they got me back up top, but there was still the matter of getting back down the trail, which was so snowed over we were plowing through snow that was waist deep. Plus, I had frostbite on my toes, which didn't help me walk."

"And the rest of your team?" Carried asked.

"Had to carry me down. Not the best way to exit your own rescue, but this is what can happen. There will be times when everything goes right, and times when nothing does."

"Did he live?" one of the students asked.

Jack nodded. "Several surgeries later, then he went back up to attempt the photo again."

"He survived that one?" Carrie asked.

Jack shrugged. "I warned him not to go. But I never got a call to come get him, so I assume he got what he was after without being mauled again."

Carrie shut her eyes to visualize Jack on that rescue. In her mind, it was a much bigger, much more difficult operation than he had described. It had to be. And she could almost picture Jack suspended in midair for all that time. Hanging there with no way up, no way down. Her stomach turned over, and not with the prospect that she might, one day, find herself in a similar situation, but with the idea that she could have lost Jack even before she'd found him. Suddenly her hands started shaking and she crossed her arms over her chest and tucked them into her armpits so he wouldn't see.

"And now," Jack said, going back to his desk

chair, "let's talk about the wildlife you'll encounter, and how to deal with it. Because you might have to rescue that guy I was talking about, and the bear may still have its paw on his chest, or its mouth on his leg."

"Good work," Jack said, several hours later, as the group of students prepared to walk back down the trail and go home. His teaching day was over and now he had several hours ahead of him at the hospital. The work had to go on, and he had to pull his weight, even though Caleb and Leanne were back now, despite the classes. Which meant his eight- and ten-hour days were now more like eighteen. But it was good. He was optimistic about the program, optimistic about his students and, more than anything, optimistic about Carrie. She'd trained three students on bouldering alongside the three he'd trained, and she'd done it like a pro.

Everything about Carrie impressed him and the more he saw of her, the more he wanted her. *As a team leader*. Maybe even, at some point, he could get her trained to teach. "How many times have you been up here practicing since we were up here?" he asked, his eyes trailing over to where they'd almost *practiced* something other than bouldering. Then he remembered where they *had* practiced. Or, actually, come close to perfection.

"Eight or ten. Sometimes once a day, sometimes twice." She tucked her gear into her bag, then picked it up and slung it over her shoulder. "I'd like to stop by and take Bella for a walk," she said. "If you don't have any plans."

"Just working. Going to cover the evening shift."

"In the ER? Because I'm down for a split shift there myself."

"Yep. And keeping my fingers crossed we're not too busy." Which maybe wasn't the best thing now that he knew Carrie was on with him. Because not busy meant more time to interact, which was exactly what he did *not* need. "So, I guess I'll see you later."

"You're going straight in?"

"After I grab something to eat. Probably pizza, since Millie's is now off my list."

"Why?"

"Janice finally asked me out. She said she wants to cook for me privately now that she knows you and I aren't..." He cringed. "Since everybody in town knows that our living arrangement didn't work. Which means that everyone thought our arrangement was an—" he arched sexy eyebrows and smiled *"—arrangement."*

Carrie laughed out loud. "And Janice tried to get in on some of that?"

"Twice, actually. She said she wanted to cook for me, and after I told her no, she suggested there might be other things I needed, or wanted."

"Poor Jack—the object of somebody's lascivious attention," she teased as they started back down the trail, side by side. "Must be tough, being you."

This was the first time they'd had any kind of interaction outside school or work, since he'd flat-out rejected her. It was nice. It felt right. Even though he didn't deserve it. What he'd done... To spend the evening in bed with her, then practically kick her out his door. No, he didn't deserve nice conversation. He didn't deserve anything.

But he'd missed her. More than he'd expected. "Look, about what I said after..."

"It's over, Jack. You know what you want, and you've never been anything but honest about it. I got a little sidetracked, but I'm back on track now, so there's nothing to say. Or apologize for. Or explain."

He wasn't sure if she was being honest or simply trying to hide behind the barriers she put up to keep herself from getting hurt. Either way, he decided it was best to leave it alone. Because he truly did not want to hurt Carrie in any way. This past week, he'd paced the floor every night, losing sleep worrying that he had.

And he still worried. This was her move to call, though. If she simply wanted to ignore what they'd done, what he'd done, that was her decision, and he would respect that.

"If that's what you want..."

"It's what I want," she said, trying to sound complacent, but reflecting something different, something almost sad in her eyes. "And we're good, I hope." She reached over and gave his arm a squeeze. "Because I've missed you."

He felt the tingle from her touch. It rushed up his arm. Caused him to gasp. Caused him to wish there could be more. But there couldn't—not of *that*. Still, he was beginning to have some hope that they could have a friendship again, because he felt better when he and Carrie were on good terms. And he was positive he could keep his feelings under control.

"So, how about grabbing a pizza with me before we go our separate ways? I don't have to be on for an hour, you don't have to be on for two, so somewhere in the middle of all that I think there's a little time for pepperoni and cheese, or do you prefer Italian sausage? Can you deal with that?"

"Are you sure about this? About us working together? Because I can always walk away and—"

"And ham. I really like ham on my pizza."

She smiled. Shook her head, and continued, "I like mushrooms, onions and peppers. Can *you* deal with that?"

"To make this *professional* relationship work, we've got to—"

"Black olives," she said.

"What?"

"I really like black olives on my pizza."

He sighed, chuckled, and smiled up at the sky. What the hell was he going to do?

They weren't even inside the pizza restaurant when Jack's phone rang. He looked to see who it was, saw the hospital switchboard number come up, and sighed. "We may be looking at a rain check on that pizza," he said, punching into his voice mail.

He listened for a few seconds, then hit the disconnect. "It's Priscilla," he said. "Another heart episode. This one's bad."

"Someone's with her?" Carrie asked, automatically taking hold of Jack's arm and leading him toward her truck. "I'll drive," she said. "And I'll also call the hospital to make sure we're covered until we get back."

"Palloton's on his way up."

"Why?" she asked, as she slipped into the driver's seat.

"He came into the hospital, looking for me.

Apparently, he's been trying to call me since he got to town, but that's when we were still up at Eagle Pointe, and there's no reception there. So he went to my house, saw I wasn't there, then headed on over to the hospital. They told him I wasn't scheduled until later but, in the meantime, if he ran into me, to tell me a call had come in from Priscilla. She was having heart problems and needed me there."

"So Palloton went?"

Jack slumped back in his seat as Carrie pushed the gas pedal to the floor. "I'm glad he did. She shouldn't be there alone."

The drive seemed interminable, but when Jack glanced over at the speedometer, he saw that Carrie was driving somewhat above the speed limit. On iced-over mountain roads. With snow starting to come down. Not much of it here, but farther up the mountain? That made him nervous. And here was a Chicago girl speeding on steep, winding, snowy mountain roads. Yet it didn't worry him as she was so competent at everything else she did, he assumed she would be as competent at road conditions many people didn't care to drive on.

"You good on snow?" he asked her, to make sure.

She nodded. "Remember where I grew up? Snow is a way of life there. I've driven in it, lived in it when I was on the street, slept in it… I know snow. Also, snow conditions were covered in my tactical training, so…no problem." Keeping her eyes on the road, she reached over and squeezed Jack's arm. "No problem at all."

He sighed, but not from relief. He was thinking of Evangeline. Wishing she'd been intrepid the way Carrie was. Their marriage may not have lasted had she not crashed. But he'd still have Alice. And, dear God, he missed his daughter so badly…

Jack turned his head to the window so Carrie wouldn't see the tears brimming his eyes. She'd found her way into so many places in his life, but not there. Nobody, nothing was there except his grief.

CHAPTER NINE

"I WASN'T SURE what to do," Palloton explained as he held the door open for Carrie and Jack. "I got her to lie down and I've been taking her pulse, which is one hundred-fifty."

Carrie cringed, then asked, "While she's lying down?" It had taken them twice as long as it should have to get there, owing to the road conditions. Icy at the start, getting worse the higher they'd got. She'd nearly slid off the road twice, turning completely around once in a spin. Good thing she was from Chicago where snow, ice and bad driving conditions were a huge thing in the winter. She was glad Jack had trusted her with that. So much so, he hadn't been as nervous about it as she'd been. He hadn't even grumbled when she'd finally called it quits, parked the truck, and told him they were going to hike the rest of the way because the truck wasn't going to make it all the way up. So they'd spent an extra half-hour on foot, cutting through some mighty tough terrain, alternately taking the lead, then helping the other along in the worst spots. He'd pull her up on one outcrop of rocks, she'd pull him up the next.

Carrying the litter that last little bit had slowed them, too. But she was glad they had it. Glad that Jack was a good teacher and had drummed that lesson into her head. That, and many more.

Getting up here—it was almost like they worked this way all the time. They'd found an unspoken rhythm and a routine that worked. It was nice. Before, in her job, it had always been on the edge of adversarial, them against her, or the other way around. But this was them, together. And it was such a good fit. Now, as they were starting on Priscilla, she only hoped their delay hadn't caused even more problems for the old woman.

Palloton nodded. "She's breathing too fast, too. I counted her respirations at about twenty-six, give or take. I don't know if she's got a fever…

I couldn't find a thermometer…but she doesn't feel hot."

Carrie looked at Jack, who was on his way to the hall. "So, what exactly is her diagnosed condition. You didn't tell me last time we were out here."

Jack paused, then turned back to Carrie. "It's an intermittent tachycardia, which would normally be treated by a beta-blocker, if my grandmother would take a beta-blocker. But I'm betting she hasn't taken one pill of her prescription."

"Paradoxical supraventricular tachycardia?" Carrie asked.

"Exactly," Jack said, arching impressed eyebrows.

"I study," she told him, as she knew most doctors didn't expect that kind of specialized knowledge from a paramedic.

"Indeed you do. So now…what?" he asked.

"She's going to need an adenosine intravenous injection before she goes into atrial fib."

"Why didn't you go to medical school, Carrie?" he asked. "Because you're good."

"No time, no money. Got myself as far as my

circumstances would allow me, and I'm happy here." She grabbed the backpack and pulled out a bag of IV solution and tubing to prepare for the procedure. "It's good work, Jack. Maybe not what I really wanted, but I like what I do."

"Have you ever considered going on for more?"

"Sometimes. And I might. Or I might not. It depends on where I finally land, I suppose. So, what do we do about getting her to the hospital? Because getting her out of here…I'm not even sure we can do that. Especially now that it's dark."

"If she'll go to the hospital," he said, turning back to the hall, then disappearing.

"She's not going to agree to any of this." Palloton stepped around Carrie on his way back into the bedroom. "She already told me she wasn't leaving here, that Jack would have to treat her where she is, because she isn't going down the side of the mountain on a stretcher."

"Is that the only alternative?"

"Maybe. I've been assessing the situation, and we don't have a lot of options. So, what's up with the truck? Can we get her that far, then drive her out?"

Carrie shook her head. "Road's too iced over. It's off the road, and there's no traction to get it back on."

"OK, well, let me see if I can figure out plan B."

Plan B… Carrie sighed as she joined Jack in the bedroom, where he was already assessing Priscilla's vital signs.

Carrie immediately went to work inserting an IV, and by the time she was finished, Jack had completed his assessment. "She's not as bad as she could be," he said gravely. "But I don't think we've got time to wait until we can get some-one up here to help get her out the proper way, which could be sometime tomorrow, after it's light again. I don't want to wait that long. I need her back at Sinclair as fast as we can to get her stabilized."

"Well, Palloton's working on a plan B."

"Plan B is never good. Especially since I al-ready know what that's going to have to be."

Carrie was afraid she did, too. "Down the side of the mountain?"

"By foot," Jack confirmed. "Even though my grandmother's going to refuse it."

"Can the three of us do that? The snow's picking up. Not bad yet, but bad enough."

"As bad as Chicago snow?" he asked, grinning.

"Chicago snow's flat on the ground. This snow is on the side of a mountain. My preference is for flat, Chicago snow any day."

Jack chuckled. "Spoken like a true city girl."

"Yeah, well, tonight you'd better hope city girl can be rugged mountain girl, because that's who you'll need to help get your grandmother out of here." She was praying she could do this. Snow wasn't the issue. Getting down the mountain in it was.

"I wish we had some kind of screw vehicle for these rescues," he said, checking his grandmother's blood pressure again.

"What's that?" Carrie asked.

Priscilla was the one to tell her. "It's a vehicle that can take on the ice and snow like nothing you ever saw. Right now I'm wishing you had one, too, 'cause I don't trust the bunch of you carrying me down on foot. I want to live to tell the tale."

"A little hike in the woods isn't going to kill you, old woman," Jack said affectionately, as he took hold of her hand and held it. "You've done worse."

"Done better, too," she said, her voice noticeably weakening. Then she nodded at Carrie. "Glad you brought her along. She's the one I'm counting on to take care of me."

Jack tightened his squeeze on his grandmother's hand. "You're going to be fine," he reassured her.

"If you don't drop me over the side of the mountain." Priscilla closed her eyes and let out a long, exhausted sigh.

Jack looked up at Carrie but didn't say a word. He didn't have to. She already knew, she'd already seen the worry in his eyes. "I think we need to start back down right away," she said.

"I know," he said. "Because her heart rate's up and her blood pressure's dropping."

She stepped up behind him and squeezed his

shoulder. "We're going to get her through this, Jack."

He stood and whispered in Carrie's ear, "If she lasts the night."

The reality of his words hit hard, and for the first time Carrie truly understood what mountain rescue was all about. It wasn't just the adrenaline rush of the climb and the excitement of going over a cliff to rescue a climber, or two days out on a search. It was about the normal things—the heart attacks, the broken legs, injuries she'd seen as a cop. But this…it scared her, and she was glad she had Jack to rely on. To pull her through it.

Palloton stepped into the doorway. "Tell me what I need to do, Wiwa."

Jack motioned Palloton and Carrie down the hall before he spoke. "Give me your opinion. Down Larson's Pass? It's longer but easier."

"Unless you want to try going over Monty's Ridge," Palloton said, "and down from there. Even with the snow and ice, it could shave off maybe half the time. And we'll be able to get cell reception quicker, which means we can have an ambulance waiting for us at the trailhead, rather than us having to wait for an ambulance since we can't call until we reach the flats, which is what'll happen if we take Larson's."

Carrie was impressed with the men's knowledge of the mountain. Not only of the mountain but all the details that could make or break a rescue. Jack wanted her to eventually lead a team, but could she ever be as good as these two? Or have the same kind of knowledge they did? "If Monty's is faster, why would you even consider something else?" she asked.

Palloton was the one to answer. "Because Jack's not sure you're up to Monty's. Beginners have no business on it."

"Can the two of you get us where we need to go in the dark?" she asked.

"We can," Jack said.

"And you want me to stay in Saka'am and be a team leader at some point?" she asked him.

"I do," he answered.

"Then, as team leader, I make the decisions. Correct?"

Jack nodded. "But not this time. I know where

this is going, and I've got to be as responsible for your life as I am for my grandmother's. You're not up to Monty's."

"Will Priscilla survive it?" she asked.

"She will, because Palloton and I know how to get her down."

"Then that's what you do. You get her down, and I'll get me down. My decision, Jack. We'll take her down Monty's. I'm not afraid of it, and I'm not afraid of being left behind, if that's what you must do. I'm perfectly capable of hunkering down for a night and getting myself back to town in the morning, if that's what it comes to." She was good in the snow, she wasn't afraid of that. Or the dark, or the cold. She'd spent years in far worse than that, and had survived. So this didn't worry her.

"Or you could stay here, at my grandmother's, until someone can come get you."

"What? And miss my first mountain rescue? Not a chance." If this was what her future life was going to be about, she was *not* going to be left behind. Even if Jack issued the order. "I'm going down with you, like it or not."

"And this is where Carrie gets insubordinate," Jack snapped, then immediately pulled back. "Sorry," he said. "I'm just worried."

"Not insubordinate, Jack," she said, sympathetic to his position. "Confident. I'm really good at trial by fire and this is where I get to prove myself."

"It's not about proving yourself, Carrie. It's about saving our patient. That's the only thing it's about."

"If you don't force me to stay back, I can do exactly what I'm supposed to."

"We don't have time to debate this, Carrie. Going down with Palloton and me means you follow orders, from either one of us. You don't go out on your own. You don't jump the scene. You do as we tell you. Do you understand that? Because I can't have—I won't have people on my team who can't follow the rules."

He was so…in command in a way she hadn't seen him before. Of course, she hadn't been in a situation like this with him before, so this was a new side of him, and she liked it. It filled her with confidence. With Jack in charge, this was going to work. And, in the meantime, she would get to show him some of *her* skills, even if he wasn't specifically looking for them. Hopefully she'd even impress him. "Yes, I understand."

"We could use her, Jack," Palloton said. "Some of those descents are pretty steep, and having three people going down them will be a big help."

He regarded her for a minute, and she couldn't read his expression. "I *can* help," she added. "You know I can."

"I know other things about you, too, Carrie. Which is why I'm hesitating."

"Well, hesitating isn't getting your grandmother out of here. So, yes or no. Do I go, do I stay?"

"If I tell you to stay, would you?"

Honestly, probably not. It would be her inclination to simply follow them, make herself ready if they needed extra help. She was sure this was what Jack was thinking. "I don't know," she finally said.

"Which leaves me no choice, does it? Look, I know you're good, and I know you want to be part of this. But don't do what you typically do, Carrie. OK?"

She nodded. "I'll do what I need to do."

"Then get yourself ready. I want to be out of here inside fifteen minutes. Down Monty's."

Monty's. She could do this. And prove to Jack she was the perfect choice to head one of his teams. He'd see that.

"She's a good one, Jack," Palloton said, as Carrie was getting Priscilla dressed for the trip. "Crazy about you. Trying as hard as she can to break through. So, if I were you…"

"It won't work. If I thought there was any chance it could…" He shook his head. "But there's not. I don't have what she needs."

"I don't think she sees it that way."

"She's in a new situation. She comes from a very difficult background. What she sees in me is a way to get past that. That's all. I represent something she wants, something she's never had, and eventually she'll recognize that she wants what I represent and not who I am."

"Or maybe she knows what she wants more

than you give her credit for. Look, I've got the stretcher ready. So as soon as Carrie gets Priscilla squared away…"

Jack nodded. Then went to see his grandmother.

"Carrie said you're taking me down over Monty's," Priscilla said, her voice weak but her smile vibrant. "She's a nice girl, Jackie. Remember that, in case anything happens. She's a very nice girl, and I approve."

"Save your breath, old woman," he said, as he took hold of her hand. "I know what you're up to and it's not going to work. She works for me. That's all there is."

Priscilla gave her grandson a wink. "I'm sure," she said. "And you don't have to do this, Jackie. I never meant to be a burden to anyone. I can face whatever happens. I'm ready."

"You're not a burden," Jack said tenderly. "A pain in the backside maybe. But not a burden."

"You're a good boy, Jackie. Always have been. And all that in the past with Evangeline…"

"Look, Priscilla, you need to save your strength. Getting you out of here isn't going to be easy, and I don't want you going into any kind of distress once we get started. So, please, just rest now. Let me do what I have to do, and before you know it you'll be at Sinclair, in a warm bed, making demands of all the nurses."

"Wouldn't it be easier to leave me here and let nature finally take her course?" the old woman asked. "I've lived a good life, Jackie. No regrets. Maybe it's time…"

Carrie, who was standing in the doorway, bit her lip to fight back tears, and glanced over at Jack, who looked almost in tears himself. Then she stepped to his side and put a supporting arm around his waist. "No way," she said, struggling to keep the quiver from her voice. "I need this experience, and I'm not going to let you ruin it for me. Jack's a strict instructor, and he'd fail me if I simply walked away. So you're going to have to put up with that bumpy ride, because I'm determined to pass his course." She tightened her squeeze around his waist. "Besides, Jack needs someone in his corner, and you're the only one he allows to get close."

"Seems like he's let you in, too," Priscilla said.

Carrie looked at Jack, then shook her head. “Not yet.” Then she pulled away and went to the bureau to look for warm socks.

“You should, Jackie. Like I said, she’s a good one.”

“So I’ve been told,” he said, then exited the room. Those demons were knocking on his door, and now wasn’t the time to face them. But Priscilla was right about one thing. Carrie was a good one. He just hoped that her own demons didn’t take her over on the hike down. This was what he’d feared, though, when he’d accepted her into the program. Now it was time for her to prove herself. He only hoped she could.

“We’ll have her cross her arms…something I’m sure you already know,” Jack told Carrie. “Then we’ll get her onto the stretcher. You and I will do the carrying at first, because I want to reserve Palloton’s strength for a couple of the areas that are going to be the most difficult to get through. And be very specific about this…I’ll lift her head first, then afterward you’ll lift her feet. Always put your strongest body on the head, because the upper torso is the heaviest. And on the way down I like to count off the steps out loud."

"Why?" she asked.

"So we can match rhythms. It makes it easier on the person you're transporting. It keeps you in sync with the other person doing the carrying so there's less jostling. It also lets them know you're with them. And because I don't like idle chatter. It distracts me."

"Sounds easy enough," she commented. This was all so easy to him. It was totally about common sense. Once again, she worried that she could never match up to what came so naturally to Jack but she so badly wanted to prove what she could do. All her life she'd had to prove herself one way or another, but this time it mattered more than anything else ever had. She wanted him to see, up close, what she'd told him she was capable of. She wanted to prove herself and while that wasn't the intent of this rescue, it was always her personal intent. Prove herself, no matter where or what.

Jack actually laughed. "I'll be daring you to say that after we get her down. Oh, and what you said to my grandmother about leaving her here…"

Carrie shook her head. "No need to say anything. I would never, ever consider leaving a patient behind, in any situation."

Jack blew out a breath. "I didn't expect you would. Anyway, let's get this thing going."

"Her vitals are holding," Carrie said. "I checked them again while I was getting her ready to go, and they're a little off but holding. I'm hoping she doesn't panic once we actually take her out of here, because that will make things worse."

"She won't," Jack said. "Priscilla knows what this is about. She's done a few of these rescues in her day, so she'll be fine. But since she's right on the borderline between moderate and severe, I went ahead and gave her an anti-arrhythmic, to help keep her stable for now."

"What about her cats?"

"Maybe I'll start a rescue organization for stray animals in my spare time, and let Priscilla's cats be my first." He smiled. "They'll be fine. It's not like I haven't come up here to take care of them before."

She knew he would. In his own, standoffish way, Jack took care of everything.

It had been an hour and the trail was getting increasingly rougher. The night was cold, the wind was blowing, and the trail was slippery. Despite it all, Carrie was still on the foot end of the stretcher, carrying her share of the load without complaint. Palloton brought up the side with the supplies, while he kept the IV bag in position while Priscilla slept, or held so still it seemed like she was.

And Jack was so antsy he wanted to jump out of his skin. He was worried…about Priscilla, about Carrie's lack of experience in these conditions. About getting off the damned mountain. That was something he *always* worried about—the details of the rescue. Because one detail skipped over, one missed step in the process… It's what kept him on the edge. Kept his mind ticking off what needed to be done. Prevented him from becoming distracted by the things over which he had no control. Like now—the ice and snow. The steep incline. The fact that this was his grandmother.

But they were making steady progress, which was good. Priscilla was hanging in there, and he wasn't discouraged. Unfortunately, the roughest part was still ahead, and getting Carrie through that worried him almost as much as getting his grandmother through it. "I need to stop for a minute," he said, blowing out an exhausted breath. "We're about to reach our first real hurdle, and I want to make sure I'm ready to tackle it."

"Which is where Palloton takes over?" Carrie asked. "Because I'm good for a little while longer, if that's what we need." She set her end of the stretcher down very gingerly, then waited until Jack had lowered his before she swooped in to do an assessment of Priscilla. Jack busied himself with the IV, while Palloton made a couple of adjustments to the stretcher.

"It gets narrow in one area, so you're going to have to bring up the rear, Carrie. I need Palloton's strength getting through there. And I can't look back to make sure you're OK. You need to understand that. If something happens, Palloton and I *will* keep going, because once we start the steepest part of the descent, there's no place to stop. This really isn't the first rescue I'd put a beginner out on, so I'm sorry about this, but this is a good example of what you'll be getting yourself into once you're out on your own."

"I'll be fine," she said. "You don't have to worry about me."

But he did. And the further into this thing they got—and he didn't mean just this rescue—the more he did. "Shout if you have to drop back or drop out. Always let your team members know what you're doing. And stay close to where you drop out, if that's what you must do, so when we come back for you, we'll know where to look. Like I said, first rule of the rescue…stay in touch." He was praying that wouldn't be the case, but this next stretch worried him. As much as he'd been up and down it, it wasn't friendly. But it cut hours off the trip, and that was what he needed. So he took a drink of water, stuck the bottle in the backpack, then handed it to Carrie, and took his place at Priscilla's feet, since he'd already carried the heaviest part of the load for the past hour.

And he kept thinking to himself that when they got down to the bottom, there were things he was going to change. A lot of things. "Ready?" he called, then braced himself as Palloton picked up his end of the stretcher and waited for Jack to do the same.

The first little bit wasn't so bad, but all too soon they came to the first hurdle, a steep descent of about twenty feet. While it wasn't a sheer drop-off, it was a challenge, especially at the top of it where the path was jagged with rocks and tree roots extended out over the trail, rather than burying themselves into the dirt below.

"You got it?" he called to Palloton, who was beginning to turn around since he'd have to elevate Priscilla's head to get her down this part, meaning he was going to have to go backward now.

"Yep," he called back, getting into position and starting to lift the stretcher.

"Can I wiggle in there somewhere to shine more light?" Carrie called out. "There's that rock just ahead, and if I can get behind it, maybe I can get up top and shine the flashlight down on the trail ahead of you."

"That takes a vertical climb in ice and snow, and you're not ready for that," Jack called back. "So just stay behind and do the best you can with the light."

"But I'm looking at the rock right now, Jack, and it doesn't seem like it would be a bad climb."

"For someone with experience, maybe not. But you don't have experience, so just follow us. OK? Don't get sidetracked by something you can't do, because if you get injured, there's not a thing I can do to help you."

"I'm capable," she muttered. "And I won't get hurt."

Jack swallowed hard. This was where he'd known he might have a problem with Carrie. Her need to do it on her own. Maybe later, when she was trained and experienced, that stubborn streak wouldn't be a bad thing. Her unwillingness to give up would save lives, he was sure of that. But getting her to that point… "But I'm not willing to risk that, Carrie, because we can't get two of you out of here, and if your injury is serious, you might die of exposure, waiting for me to get back to rescue you. So, no. Direct order. *Don't do it.* Do you understand me? I don't want you attempting anything other than what I tell you to do."

"Fine," she said, huffing out an impatient breath.

He heard it, and smiled. She was a handful for sure. In a personal way, he liked that. Liked the challenge. Liked it that she always kept him on his toes. But professionally…

It was so frustrating not being able to contribute to this rescue in any substantial way. She could have gotten up that rock. She looked at it. It might have plenty of places to grab hold of, and she was certainly strong enough to pull herself up if she could find the right spot. After all, she'd become pretty good at the dead hang and horizontal climbing. And this would be a combination of both, only going up, not sideways. The light she could have given them from up there might cut ten or fifteen minutes off this part of the descent. It was a tricky one, she knew. But if they could only see the next step in front of them…

But no. She was bringing up the rear. Carrying medical supplies. Watching. Doing nothing. Actually, right now she was sitting on a rock, waiting, while they were trying to figure out how to get Priscilla down the next drop-off.

Carrie shone her light over on the rock she wanted to scale. There were so many advantages to this rescue if she could get up there… Standing, she walked across the narrow path, her light still shining on it. To explore it. Nothing else. And the front side didn't seem to have everything she might have liked to climb it, but maybe around back…

She took a step off the path, then another and another…looking for the perfect spot. Not that she intended to climb. But still…

Shining her light right then left, she surveyed that rock like an art connoisseur might survey a masterwork, until… "Yes," she said under her breath, taking several more steps to the rear, holding her flashlight in one hand and sliding her hand along the rock face with her other. It was damp. More like slick from a thin film of ice. Something she was positive Jack or Palloton could tackle.

She looked up at the top of the rock. It wasn't so far. Maybe twenty or twenty-five feet. She'd scaled walls that high in her cop training. But this rock…yes, Jack could do it. Easily.

She closed her eyes for a moment and pictured him. His strength. His determination. He would climb this rock if it aided the rescue, she thought. He absolutely would. And if he got angry with her for discovering that, well…she could deal with it. She had from her superiors before. And Jack…he simply didn't know what she could do. She hoped her little jaunt off the path would all blow over once she told him what she'd discovered. Besides, with Priscilla's life hinging on getting her to the hospital as quickly as possible…

No more thinking. She was going back to the trail to have another go at him. To try to convince him that he could have the light he needed for the next leg of this. Now that she'd seen what she'd have to do, and understood it, she had no doubt. So it was about convincing Jack to do it, or let her…that was the biggest hurdle, not the rock.

Carrie started her trip back to the path, maybe too eagerly, because she wasn't even halfway there when she took a misstep and twisted her ankle. Dropping to her knees, she slipped sideways in the snow and ice, right down a little embankment. She kept rolling, even though she fought to reach out and grab hold of something…anything. But there was nothing to help her. Nothing at all, until she hit the bottom with a thud so hard it knocked the breath out of her, and her voice. No way to get to Jack now. Not even to call out to him as she grappled to breathe again.

So, there she was. Alone, in trouble. Snow coming down on her. Her ankle throbbing. Her back aching. Not even sure if she'd broken any bones or not. Right where Jack had expected her to end up.

Discouraged, and still breathing hard, Carrie shut her eyes. In a minute she'd have to brace herself to stay there. Right now, all she wanted to do was cry. And she did. Quietly. Not even aware that her tears were freezing on her eyelashes.

* * *

"Sorry, Jack. There's no sign of her."

Palloton had been out looking for ten minutes while he'd stayed behind with his grandmother. "No tracks?"

"If there were, I couldn't see them."

"The medical bag?"

Palloton help it up. "Sitting on a rock about twenty feet back."

Slowly, Jack stood up, looked around, even though he couldn't see much of anything. He hated this. Hated the decision he was going to make. Hated that even though he'd told her not to go up on that rock, he was sure she had. God only knew what had happened to her in the process.

"What did she think she was doing?" he asked. "Why didn't she tell us where she was going, or call out when she got herself in trouble?"

"Maybe she couldn't, Jack. Accidents happen out here."

"And stubbornness." Something he didn't want to think about but couldn't dismiss. Sighing heavily, he finally said, "We've got to go on.

We've stayed here too long, and Carrie…" His voice cracked. "She knew the consequences if she went off on her own."

Palloton stepped up behind him and patted him on the shoulder. "We'll come back up at first light. Carrie knows how to take care of herself, so she'll be fine until then."

He hoped so. And that was all he had to hang on to as they made their way down the mountain, and the only sounds he could hear were the crunching of snow under their boots and the interminable counting. What he wanted to hear was Carrie. But he didn't. And he knew that after he squared his grandmother away at the hospital, the worst was yet to come.

Tonight, he hated this. Hated every bit of it. He'd failed Evangeline and she'd died. And he'd failed Carrie. He should have insisted that she stay back. Tried hard than he did. Watched her better. And now she…

He swallowed hard, refusing to think the last. He had a rescue to complete and nothing else mattered. Even though his heart was pounding so frantically it felt like it was about to explode.

* * *

Carrie found a tree that would shelter her from some of the snow and dragged herself up under it. She pulled down a couple of low-hanging branches to cover herself with, then sat upright to keep as much of herself off the icy ground as she could, and to help fight off sleep, then she pulled herself tight into a ball. This was her night, and this was the only way she knew how to survive it. She'd read it in Jack's notes. She'd skipped ahead of the class and read all the way through everything he'd written, and now, she was relying on it to keep her alive.

Still, why had she put herself in this spot? Why did she always put herself in some kind of bad spot? She didn't mean to be insubordinate. She only ever wanted to help. Tonight, she'd wanted to prove to Jack that she could be valuable to him. Which had landed her here. And probably without a position in his program, as well. Because he wouldn't back down from what he'd said about not allowing people in who couldn't follow orders. He was right. He couldn't. So why had she done this? Why did she always mess up?

"Because I don't trust myself to hang on to what I get after I get it." Because she'd always wanted what she didn't have, and when she finally did get it, she put up walls to keep it in, to guard it jealously. Like her ambition. And her successes. She got arrogant about them. Or was she merely insecure? Because if she ever gave in to admitting she had so much to learn, she'd realize how much she still didn't know. In a life where not knowing resulted in bad things happening, she couldn't let that happen.

So she fought everyone who threatened to show her how much she didn't know, which was only fighting herself. But she wasn't in that life now. It was her past, and she had to keep it there or she'd forever be looking for something she wouldn't find. Her stability. Her happiness. Her true belief in herself. The kind of belief Jack had had in her until now. *Until now…*

Thinking about that made her sad. And angry at herself. And very, very scared because this time there was no one to blame but herself. Before, it had been her mother, her foster parents, her supervisor, her lifestyle. Everything but her had caused her misery. Tonight she was the only one who'd caused it. This time, though, the hurt wasn't going to go away or be put aside when she took on something else. This time she'd hurt herself in a way that wouldn't heal.

Carrie swallowed hard. No arguments now. She'd accept what she had to. And move on. But wiser, she hoped. It hurt so much all she wanted to do was curl up in a ball and hope he didn't find her, hope she wouldn't have to face him. Hope she could get out on her own, grab Bella, then slip out of town so Jack wouldn't be forced into making a decision she knew he wouldn't want to make.

The thought of putting him in that position made her feel so sick to her stomach that she vomited. Then she wiped her mouth on her sleeve, dropped her head onto her knees and cried for all the things she hadn't done, and for all the things she had. She also cried for her failure because, for the first time, she was admitting she had failed. Failed miserably. And she didn't know how, or if, she could turn back from that.

Most of all, she cried for the loss of her dream—a future with Jack. It was gone. Completely, totally gone.

CHAPTER TEN

"SHE'S EXACTLY THE reason why I want to set up several teams to cover the whole area," Jack said, looking up the path he and Palloton had descended the night before. "For people who think they know what they're doing when they don't."

Like Carrie, unfortunately.

And while he was trying to hold back his judgment since he didn't know what had happened back up on the mountain, he didn't have a good feeling about anything. Not about why she'd gone missing. Or why she'd deliberately gone against his orders. Or if she was hurt. Or worse. Nothing made him feel good or optimistic. But he was ready to face it, to do what had to be done.

"Well, it's going to take us a while to get up there, since it's a whole lot worse now than it was last night." Palloton slung a hank of rope over his shoulder and waited until Jack had laced up his hiking boots before he picked up his end of the empty litter. "Litter's packed?" he asked.

"With everything we'll need to get her back down."

"Maybe she can hike," Palloton said.

"She's injured," Jack replied. "Or else she would have already made it down on her own, one way or another. She's stubborn like that. Which is why I believe she's..." No, he wasn't going to think it. Wasn't going to think anything except how to pull this rescue off. "I'm glad you're the one going back up there with me, buddy. I don't think I could do this with anybody else."

"Well, I've got a wager for it," Palloton said, adjusting his backpack and following Jack to the path that would take them back up.

"Of course you would. So what is it? And what do I have to ante up?"

"Your heart and soul."

"And you?"

"The knowledge that you're doing the right thing."

But was he? Or could that even happen because he couldn't keep her in the program. Not now. That was one hard and fast rule he couldn't break, part of the hospital's rule, and he couldn't go against that. Not for Carrie. Not even if he loved her. "First things first. Let's hope she stayed put, like I told her to do if we got separated." Yeah, right. Carrie following orders? No way in hell that would happen.

"So, what are you going to do about her, Wiwa, once we find her? Because, admit it or not, you're in love with her."

"Mind your own damn business," Jack said, with absolutely no fight or animosity in his voice. The truth was, he was scared. He didn't know how he was going to face this if… "Ready?" he asked, leaving the flats to begin the climb.

"Look, Jack. My business, right now, is watching your back. And that's going to be hard to do if you're distracted by your feelings for her. So get your head in the right place. Admit your feelings instead of fighting them, because if you don't, you're going to be brooding about this the whole way up. And a brooding rescuer isn't a good rescuer."

Palloton was right, of course. Maybe if he said the words out loud, they would stop rattling around in his head, disturbing him, confusing him. "I might have some feelings," he said. "Not that it's going to matter once I do what I have to do with her."

"You always make things too complicated," Palloton said, as he nudged the litter forward. "Remember that time when we…"

Carrie examined her ankle and decided it wasn't broken. It hadn't swollen up any more than it had last night, the pain hadn't changed, and she could grit her teeth and range it in small circles. That was good. What wasn't good was the snow. She'd kept it off her most of the night.

She was so light-headed, though. And cold… so cold. Drowsy, too. Sleep had overtaken her a couple times against her will, and she was fighting it off right now. Plus, it was getting more and more difficult to concentrate and to breathe. All signs of hypothermia. Bad signs. Sighing, she repeated the words she'd repeated over and over for the past couple hours, to assess her speech pattern, hoping she wouldn't start slurring. "Your hypothalamus is your brain's temperature-control center. Its purpose is to raise body temperature by triggering the things that heat and cool the body. Then there's also vatho…vatho…"

Damn. She swallowed hard, and concentrated on that one single word.

"Vatho…" *Vaso...vaso...* Not vatho.

It was closing in on her. She could hear it. The slurring was now starting. After that, what? She tried to pull the answer from her memory, but couldn't quite grasp it. Was confusion or memory loss part of the process? She couldn't remember.

Shifting positions against the tree that had protected her all night, she laid her head back against it and shut her eyes. She wanted to sleep so badly. Just a minute or two, she promised herself. "Your hypothalamus is your brain's… what?" She couldn't remember. In fact, the only thing she could remember was Jack, and it was his face she could see so clearly when she finally gave herself over to sleep.

* * *

Jack wasn't in the mood to talk on their ascent, and Palloton respected that by keeping quiet himself. Occasionally, one or the other called out Carrie's name, hoping to hear a response from her but not expecting it. They'd climb for several minutes, then stop at every point that could have been a falling-off place for her. Because, yes, Jack did expect she'd gone off the trail somewhere. So he scouted left when they stopped, while Palloton scouted right. Then they switched, eventually meeting back up on the trail and moving forward a little farther. Stop, repeat, then move on.

It was a damn slow process, but right now it seemed slower than it ever had before. "I'm betting she's up at the rock she wanted to climb," Jack said, discouraged by the idea that it was still a good hour ahead of them at a normal pace. And in the snow, and they had to stop every few yards to look around.

"Then I say we go straight there," Palloton suggested. "Trust your gut. Besides, the other team is bringing up the rear, should be about thirty minutes behind us, and they can cover the rest of the way up while we go on."

Jack blew out an icy, discouraged breath. "I hate this," he said. "It was like that day…" Like the day Evangeline died, he almost said. But he didn't because he wasn't worthy to speak her name. But that day played in his mind now: the knock on the door that had woken him out of a sound sleep; the heavy rain; the drive out to the spot where her car had gone over. And the waiting… the damned, interminable waiting. And hoping.

"Nobody blames you, Jack. It was one of those unfortunate accidents. I know things were said to you at first, but people changed their minds when they got over the shock."

Accusations. People saying how everybody knew that Evangeline hated to make that drive herself. That it was dangerous, that it scared her. That he shouldn't have let her do it. *Like he shouldn't have let Carrie make the trip back down with them last night.* That he shouldn't have worked thirty-six hours without sleep, otherwise he'd have been able to fulfill his promise to drive Evangeline. That he should have stopped her when he knew how bad the weather was, like he should have stopped Carrie.

Yes, people had said things…the same things he'd thought all those hours when he'd sat at the side of the road, waiting for other rescuers to bring Evangeline and Alice up out of the ravine.

"But I didn't change *my* mind," Jack replied bitterly. "And everything they said was true. Every damn word of it." Words that still spun around and around in his brain.

Words that stayed with him as he and Palloton picked up their pace to get to the first steep drop-off where they could last account for Carrie.

That was where she had to be. In his heart, he knew she was there, but he didn't want any feelings of Carrie in his heart. Too late, though. She was there, despite how hard he'd tried to keep her out. Unfortunately, the minute he found her, if she was still alive, that would all end. That was the only way it could be. The only way he would have it.

The predicted hour up took two, but when they reached the place where'd she'd said she wanted to climb the rock, they stopped, and Jack immediately called her name, as Palloton prepared to explore the front face of the rock, while Jack took the back. "Carrie, can you hear me?"

He strained his ears to hear her, or anything, but it was so still, the only sound that split the air was that of his labored breathing. "Carrie!"

"Carrie!" Palloton called out from a little farther down the trail.

Jack called one more time, but knew that if she was somewhere near here, she wasn't conscious. At least, he hoped that's how far her condition had gone. *Get it together*, he told himself. *This is a rescue, it doesn't matter who it is*. But it did matter, and as he headed off the trail, all he could think of was how much it mattered.

Five, maybe ten minutes into exploring the area, he saw a lump in the snow that warranted a better look. It didn't strike any kind of hope in him because he'd learned a long time ago that the leads he came across in a search usually didn't amount to anything. But still… "You OK over there?" he called out to Palloton, as he made his way through a snow drift to the thing he wanted to explore.

"Fine. Not seeing anything, and if I go any farther I'm going to have to do some climbing down. Rather wait for you to come over here before I do that."

"Then meet me on this side," Jack yelled as he finally reached the lump. He bent down, shoved back the snow and... "Now," he yelled urgently. "I've got Carrie's bag."

Picking it up, he stood, then looked around but didn't see her. But he did see the ravine. *Another damned ravine.* Another woman he loved. "I may have something," he said, taking care not to get too close to the edge, lest it give way and he fell.

"On my way, Wiwa," Palloton called, and within a couple of minutes he was standing by Jack's side, looking down, as well.

"She's got to be down there," Jack said. "Given the proximity of her backpack..." He lifted his protective goggles, as if that would give him a better look, then turned to his friend. "I've got to go down," he said.

"Well, I've got everything packed on the litter—helmet, harness, crampons, rope. Top-roping, I assume."

"Yeah," Jack said, getting into his gear. "It shouldn't be very far down, and if she's there, we're going to have to get her up. So that's probably the best way to go." It was slower than free climbing, which was simply taking on the rock without the aid of equipment. But he needed the steadying of Palloton on a second rope at the top, and because they'd done this hundreds of times before, they had their own rhythm. So Palloton fixed the ropes as Jack secured an anchor in the ground, then strapped on his own medical bag. "If she's down there, radio the other team to come up, because we're going to need some strength to lift her out."

"She's going to be fine, Jack," Palloton said, as Jack stepped to the edge, turned around, and prepared to go down.

Rather than replying, Jack pulled the goggles back over his eyes and lowered himself off the edge, found his footing, and started his descent. It didn't take long, even in the snow, as the drop-off wasn't very steep. But if she'd fallen over it… "Carrie," he called out the instant his feet hit solid ground. "Are you down here? Can you hear me?"

"Anything?" Palloton called from up top.

"Not yet." But he was looking. Taking only a few steps at a time, then stopping and looking at everything within his view. She was here. His heart was still telling him that. But more, his instinct was telling him the same thing, and in a rescue, instinct always counted. He trusted it more than he did his heart. "Carrie," he called again, then looked. Nothing. Not a sound. No sight of her. So he moved and did the same thing, then did it again and again until…

Had he heard something? Something besides his own breathing?

"Carrie?" he called out, taking in a deep breath, then holding it so he could hear everything around him. And sure enough…a moan. Very faint, very brief. But it was the most beautiful sound he'd ever heard.

"She's down here," he called up to Palloton.

"Let the other team know she's alive and we've got to move fast."

Which was exactly what he did. He picked up his pace, heading in the direction from which her moan had come. He was fighting the snow, fighting the ice, the rocks, the tree limbs…all the obstacles in his way until he saw her, huddled up in a fetal position. She was covered in branches, her back to a tree. Smart, he thought immediately. Just the way he'd have taught her, when they got to that lesson. That was Carrie's instinct at work. A very good instinct. He was proud and sad all at the same time because it was also an instinct that wouldn't get tested again under his supervision.

"Not sleeping," she said to him when he reached her and dropped to his knees in the snow. "Hypothermic, but not sleeping. You wouldn't let me," she whispered, as Jack pulled her close and hugged her at first, then went into doctor mode to examine her.

"You *are* going to fire me, aren't you?" she asked, as he took her blood pressure.

"Yes," he said gently, as her pressure registered low but not dangerously so.

She looked over at him, attempted a half-frozen smile, and said, "I knew you would. It's what I'd do, too, with someone like me." Then she finally shut her eyes and went completely to sleep.

"I love you," he said, giving her a kiss on her cold forehead. Of course, she didn't hear that, which was fine with Jack, because he didn't want her to. There was no point. Absolutely no point.

"Priscilla's fine," Jack said, pulling up a chair and sitting next to Carrie's hospital bed. "The trip down the mountain was pretty rough on her… lots of bruises. And she's complaining about that, but not as much as I thought she would. Also, I think she's ready to move to civilization. Not sure how that's going to work…there's a house about a mile down the road from me coming up for sale, so I might grab it for her."

"And her cats?" Carrie asked, trying to sound interested, even though she wasn't. Right now, nothing interested her other than the fact she had no place to go once she was out of the hospital, and nothing to do.

"Plenty of room." He settled back, crossed one leg over the other, and looked straight at her. "So, do you want to talk about it?"

"What's there to talk about? You gave me an order, I disobeyed it, I got myself into trouble, and I should pay the price for that. No blame, Jack. It's what you have to do and I'm good with it."

"But I want to know why you did it, Carrie."

"You mean disobey your order, Jack?"

He nodded.

"I didn't. Not really. What I did was to go look for a way to get up that rock, but I wasn't actually going to climb it. I wanted to show you it could be done. That there was a way. And I thought, well…maybe since you didn't want me doing the climbing, if I could find the way, maybe you or Palloton would go up and leave me to the carrying. That's how I've always been, Jack, trying to find something better. And I haven't hidden my past from you. You knew that was in me."

She shut her eyes, grappling for the right

words. "I know I shouldn't have gone off the way I did. But that's me, and apparently I haven't overcome that in myself. I still need to prove everything. Prove I'm better or smarter or more capable than anybody else. But not because it matters to them. Because it still matters to *me*. I always feel like..." She swallowed hard, and her lower lip trembled.

"I always feel like I'm only a step or two away from sliding right back into my other life. No matter what I do, no matter how hard I work, it won't let me go. Just like your past life won't let you go. And I'm sorry about that, Jack. For both of us. But spending that night up there alone gave me a lot of time to think, a lot of time to come to terms with what I was doing, and why. Before, when I was a cop, it was only *my* life, and that didn't matter so much. But this time it was you, Palloton...Priscilla."

"Your life matters, Carrie. I can't relate to where you come from, and I truly don't understand the kind of struggles you faced to get yourself where you are now, but you're a smart, capable woman who has so much worth and potential, and I'm only sorry you can't see that. But you're right. I know what it's like to be blinded by your past. So much so that moving forward is too difficult. Sometimes you're on the right path, but as often as not you're on the wrong one, trying to prove to yourself that you really do belong here, or you do have worth."

"Your wife and daughter?" she asked, swatting back a tear sliding down her cheek.

"I don't talk about them. I haven't. Not to anyone since… But, yes. My wife and daughter." He turned his head away, shut his eyes. "Evangeline and Alice."

Carrie didn't say anything. This was about Jack now. Maybe for the first time, what she needed to do was put someone else before herself. Not dwell in her world but try to understand his. So she waited until he spoke again, which took several minutes.

"That's the first time I've said their names aloud since they died," he finally said.

"I noticed you don't have any pictures of them in your cabin."

"Pictures are reminders, and I didn't want to be reminded."

She understood that. There was nothing in her past she wanted to be reminded of. But the more she resisted the reminders, the more she was reminded. "Of what? That you loved them?"

He finally looked straight at her. "I did. And I do."

"But you hold on to a lot of blame." He blamed himself, and she blamed others. It was a habit, a very detrimental one but one she knew they both needed to let go.

"All the blame. I didn't want to marry Evangeline in the first place. We were friends. That was all. But we decided to cross that line to see what would happen, and what happened was Alice. So we married, and I was happy enough. Not ecstatically, but it worked. I loved Alice with all my heart, and grew to love Evangeline in a different kind of way. But it was never passionate or exciting, and after a while I realized how much I missed that."

"You cheated on her?"

Jack shook his head. "Not in the traditional

sense. More like I went on a work frenzy just to keep my mind off what I was missing. To fill the void. And in doing that, I simply quit trying to connect to Evangeline. I took her for granted. And she didn't deserve that, because she tried so hard to be what I needed. I would never have cheated on her, though. That's not in my makeup. But I really should have divorced her so she could be free to find the kind of man she needed to make her truly happy. Except I didn't. Instead, I kept working, kept ignoring everything."

"Meaning you gave up on your marriage?" Carrie asked.

"Pretty much. In fact, I told her she should leave me, that she was too good to be saddled with the likes of me. But she wanted to keep trying, for Alice's sake. So I agreed. But I didn't change. I don't think I even tried. I mean, what I had was fine. Not great, but good enough. And I really did want to do what was best for my daughter. Traditional ways to Evangeline meant a two-parent family, so I respected that, even though I didn't necessarily agree with it.

"Anyway, I'd promised to take her to the reservation. She was a social worker and she had a client to see there. But she hated making that drive. So I told her I'd drive her. Except I didn't. I chose to sleep in. I told her to postpone her appointment or wait until I was awake. I'd worked thirty-six hours straight, knowing I had to make that drive, knowing that she had an appointment with a client she'd been trying to arrange for weeks. But as usual, I'd worked hard, needed to catch up on some sleep, and what was important to her wasn't important enough to me to help her.

"To cut a long story short, I slept, she made the drive on her own in the rain. And she crashed and died. Alice died a few days later. Now here I am, five years later, still having nightmares, still not able to face what I did. So when it comes to self-worth issues, I know them all because what I did cost the lives of my wife and daughter."

"It was an accident."

"And I was a better driver than Evangeline."

"You were tired."

"Because that was my way of avoiding reality. See, Carrie, I have all the excuses because I caused it. There's no other way to look at it. You jumped your scene, I ran away from mine."

"But you came back. Was that because you finally wanted to face up to it?"

"I don't know," he said. "I honestly don't know. I've told people it was because my mother needed me to take over for her, but that's not really the truth since Caleb and Leanne Carsten are here, and Sinclair Hospital has a nice list of part-time doctors who will come in on a regular basis. So, while my mother did ask me to come help for a little while, I was the one who chose to turn that *little while* into an indefinite stay. And I really don't know why."

"Maybe because it was time. I faced that on the mountain the other night, Jack. My time. My own truths. So, maybe that's why you're here now, because staying meant that, at some point, you'd have to go to Saka'am again. Like I said, maybe it was your time, too."

"Could be," he agreed. "Or maybe it wasn't about the time so much as the proximity."

"To what?" she asked.

"You," he said quite simply.

"I heard what you said to me up there on the mountain," she said. "That you love me."

"Because I do, and I shouldn't, and I can't."

"Why not?" Nothing good was going to come of this. She knew that. But she had to know if she'd done something wrong other than the obvious. It was closure, she supposed. He'd just pronounced the end to something that had never got started and now she wondered if something could have come of it. Because she loved him. Wanted to be more *for him*, to be better, to think of him first…to think of him all the time. Even though she'd never known what love was, that had to be it. And it was something she'd never thought would happen to her. But being with Jack, taking care of him, being everything for him, *that* was what she wanted love to be.

Except it wasn't what he wanted. But she wasn't going to put up her walls this time. She wasn't going to try to come out on top because losing him was at the very bottom. The worst. The ache she knew was only going to get worse once she left Marrell. And there was no deflecting it because the pain was very real, and she was starting to feel it.

"What could I offer you?" he asked. "Unresolved issues, a life I haven't come to terms with yet? You need better than that, Carrie."

"But don't you think I should have some say in what I need?" OK, so the fighter in her wasn't quite ready to give up. Maybe that was one of her positive attributes after all. Because she didn't want to give up on *this* before she'd had a chance to experience it. "Jack, you fired me from your program, which is what you had to do. I came to Marrell to find another life, because that's what I had to do. I may have some backlash from my past going on, but I do know what I need and want, and that's you. You're the only one. Ever."

"You'd stay in Marrell with me?"

"If you want me to, yes."

"But only as an experiment? Only as a way to improve yourself?"

She shook her head. "No experiments, Jack. This time I want the real thing. And the only way to improve myself is by having you there to help me."

"Like help you make coffee?" he asked, smiling, then reaching across to take her hand.

"I'm willing to learn. Anything. Everything. I mean, I know we've both got a lot of things to deal with before we know what we'll get on the other end of it, but wouldn't it be easier if we were dealing with it together? And I'm not suggesting marriage. But maybe building on the knowledge that I love you and you love me. That's got to take us somewhere better than where we both are right now, doesn't it?"

"You're willing to take that risk with me, knowing what you know?"

"You were a good man trapped in a bad situation. I know what being trapped that way is like. I also know we do things we might not normally do because we don't know where to turn, where to get help. You were trying your best, but the results were horrible. I was trying my best but the results were misguided. We're human. We have our weaknesses. And I'm so sorry for what happened to you. But you didn't cause it, much as you want to think you did. Someday maybe you'll understand that. Or maybe you won't. But you don't have to suffer it alone anymore. I know who you are, and I love who you are. And I don't consider you a risk.

"So, now I have to ask you—are you willing to take a risk with me, knowing what you know? Because I am a risk, Jack. You saw that. You know what I do." She patted the bed beside her, then scooted over to make room for him. "And I'll always work hard to get what I want. Which, right now, is you."

"No hard feelings about me kicking you out of the program?" he asked, as he sat down next to her.

"We'll talk about that later," she said, smiling. "After I've proved that I'm good enough for you to take me back in."

"That's your goal?"

"One, among many. Oh, and putting a roof over Bella's head."

"You're not going to let that dog sleep in bed with us, are you?"

"Her name's Bella. And she can sleep next to the bed. But you're going to have to be the one to tell her."

"You think so?"

"What I think is getting back together with your friends is a good thing. I'm still a paramedic, and I'm still going to keep my job at the hospital, which means when you go out to Saka'am, and you will, I'll be there with you."

"And Bella, of course."

That was the first time he'd ever said her name, which gave Carrie so much hope for so many things in their future. She would be there to help him through the rough spots when the sad memories from Saka'am overtook him. Which they would. And he would be there to help her. That was what love was about. Finally, she knew. Without a shadow of a doubt, she knew, and understood. "And Bella," she said.

"I need to go out there tomorrow," he said. "There's something I have to do. Would you be up to going with me?"

She nodded. She didn't ask why. Deep down, though, she knew. And it would be a very difficult journey to the cemetery for him, but she would be there to help him. Because she did love him. "So, about taking the risk…"

"My biggest risk is not doing this." Then he kissed her, and held her. And loved her the way no one ever had. Or ever would.

"Do you think he'll come in?" she asked Jack, as she watched Chief Charley stand in the road outside the community center. His arms were folded across his chest, and his face had the same stoic expression he always wore.

"Palloton invited him but he wouldn't commit to it, so who knows?"

Carrie looked inside to the community room, where everyone from Saka'am had crammed into every available space, and where her few friends from Marrell had also found their spots. It was a wedding day like nothing she'd ever planned. No wedding dress. No flowers. Just people…people who cared. All dressed casually. And that was all that mattered. This was her life now. This was where she finally belonged.

In a few weeks Jack would start another program, and she would be in it. Then she would come to Saka'am three days a week and do what she needed to do. In a while, she would head her own rescue team. Then someday…maybe a child. They hadn't talked about that too much yet. His memories of Alice were still too painful and she wasn't sure he was ready. But they had time. And each other. And such a good life ahead of them.

Her dream. The nice dream she'd thought she'd never have. She was ready for it. No more moving on for Carrie Kellem, soon to be Hanson. This was her life.

"You ready?" Jack asked, taking hold of her hand.

She glanced over her shoulder again at Chief Charley. "Will he be OK?" she asked.

"I hope so," Jack said.

She nodded, then looked up at Jack and smiled. "I'm ready. Now, tell me how we're going to get through all these people to get to the front." There was no aisle. Just people standing shoulder to shoulder, looking at them. Smiling. Happy.

"Got that covered," Jack said, then raised his voice. "Could you make room for us? I've got to marry this lady today."

With that, everybody stepped aside, and Mary

Whitestone begin to play a tradition Salish song on the piano while her husband, Ben, drummed the rhythm. Jack handed Carrie over to Palloton to walk her down the aisle, while he went forward to take his spot.

"It's a good thing," Palloton whispered in her ear, as they began the slow march forward.

"I know," she said, smiling. Halfway up to the front, she stopped and turned back to the door, where Chief Charley was standing. Not inside. But close enough to watch. And not smiling. But not frowning either. It was a little thing, she knew. But it was part of Jack's healing. And Chief Charley's, too. Which made a perfect wedding day even better.

She didn't smile at Charley but gave him a nod of recognition, then turned back to look at Jack. Yes, this was a really perfect day because she was truly, for the first time in her life, home.

* * * * *